Voices drift across the void,

Seeking out an open mind.

Love, loss and tragedy,

Are the ties that bind.

And if, a day should come to pass,

When you hear strange words,

And look around to find you are

Sat at home alone.

Do not fear, well, not too much,

Just harken to their verse,

And wonder what you would do,

If the positions

Were reversed?

Voices Across The Void

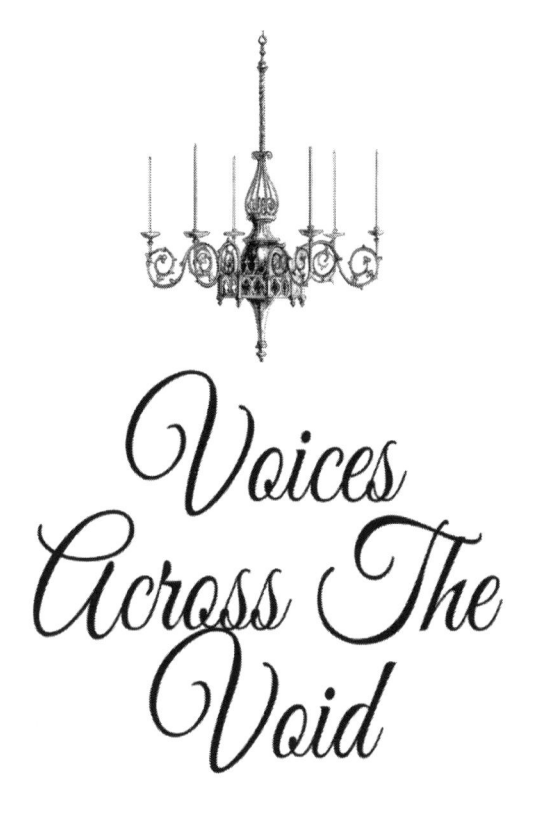

A Collection Of Ghostly Tales

By Paula Acton

All characters and events in this publication are fictitious and any resemblance to actual persons, living or dead, is purely coincidental.

This book is sold subject to the conditions that it shall not, by way of trade or otherwise, be lent, resold, hired out or otherwise circulated without the author's prior written consent in any form of binding or cover other than that in which it is published and without a similar condition being imposed upon the subsequent purchaser or reproduced in any format without written consent from the author.

Copyright ©2016 by

Paula Acton

The moral right of the author has been asserted.

Cover Artwork ©2012 by Melchelle Designs

Contents

Dedication	Pg 5
Empty	Pg 7
The Library	Pg 28
The House	Pg 46
The Cottage	Pg 58
The Broadcast	Pg 108
The Shades	Pg 149
The Elevator	Pg 170
The Hospital	Pg 184
The Bluebell Woods	Pg 200
Wake Me Up	Pg 218
The Anniversary	Pg 229
The Last Word	Pg 232
About The Author	Pg 239

DEDICATION

Sometime in life you come across a person or story that makes you stop and think about your own life. I heard about Charlie through his great uncle, he a friend I got to know playing a game on Facebook, one day he told me and other friends about his great nephew and the devastating news that he had been diagnosed with cancer. Over the next eighteen months along with people from all round the world I followed Charlie's fight, the ups and downs, the times we thought he had won his battle and finally the tragic news that he had passed away.

His parents Fiona and Joey shared their precious son with hundreds of thousands of people on Facebook, but they did more than that, in his name they created a legacy worthy of their beautiful son. Stem cells from a donated cord in the USA gave them extra precious time with their boy, and in his memory, they created Cord4Life a registered charity, sadly they recently decided that they could not continue with the charity.

Charlie's courage and strength encouraged me during a time when things in my own life were hard, he was only a little younger than my own son, and I was acutely aware of how lucky I was and how trivial my own problems were in comparison. Although no two people suffer in the same way nor can it ever be truly said one person's worries are comparable to another's, the way they deal with their troubles makes a world of difference and in this respect Charlie and his family are a shining example.

While I do not expect to make a fortune from this book, a percentage of the profits will be donated to Clic Sargent in his name.

In memory of a beautiful spirit

who always smiled

through his pain

Charlie Harris-Beard

25/06/2010 - 08/02/2013

EMPTY?

She stood with her back to the fireplace, resting against the rough stone, arms stretched out either side of her along the mantel. The asking price was more than she had wanted to pay, a lot more, buying this house would stretch her already strained finances beyond breaking point.

The problem was, she had fallen in love with the place the first time she viewed it, she had left that day, and sat with a calculator, until she could no longer fool herself it was anything more than a dream. She had put in an offer, so far below the asking price she knew the owner would view it as an insult but she had to at least know she had tried, she had not been shocked when it was rejected. Nowhere she had viewed since had changed her opinion that she was meant to have this house.

Yesterday the estate agent had called, was she still interested? She had almost deafened the poor bloke in her excitement, ten thousand off the asking price was still way over budget and her hopes had crashed back to earth at an even higher velocity than they had been raised.

It was the estate agent who suggested this second viewing, she almost refused, convinced walking away twice would be more than she could bear. The last hour had been spent leaning on the island in the centre of the kitchen, alternating between scribbled numbers, crossed out and reworked, and phone calls to her parents and bank manager. The final figure scrawled at the bottom of the page was still twenty thousand below the new asking price, she had been deflated, short of selling her car, which had she not needed it for work, she might very well have done, she could think of no other option.

The estate agent had stepped outside now to ring his client, but she could not imagine that there would be any amount of persuasion that could stop her having to face disappointment again.

She would have laughed if any of her friends had talked about a potential home in the terms she did this one in her head. To have actually put her feelings into words, tangible feelings would have been near on impossible, the closest she could come was a feeling of home, and that the house somehow wanted her here. There was a physical connection, almost like the shock from static build up, but rather than a brief flash of pain this was a warmth that made her want to linger. Stood as she was now, she could almost feel the warmth and energy travelling from the wood through her skin, reaching deep down into her soul. It was like the house had tested her and she was found worthy.

The door opened and the estate agents presence drew her back from her musings. Her heart sank seeing his face, but confusion took over as she listened to his words. Her new offer had been rejected but the seller had accepted her previous offer which had been five thousand below the one she had just submitted, something to do with a reoccurring dream, he had been meaning to contact the agent himself to sort it out.

The estate agent himself seemed as dazed and confused as she was but eventually it began to sink in, the house was hers, and was hers at a price that would not force her to borrow from her parents and live on beans on toast for the foreseeable future. She was not sure who was more shocked when in an explosion of joy, she let out a whoop and threw her arms round the agent, only when she released him did she notice the tears of joy dripping from her face and onto the wooden floor. She did not notice the pink tinge they glowed with before they were quickly absorbed into the timber.

Weeks passed quickly, as there was no chain the sale process was relatively painless, though of course there were still the usual reports to be got, papers to sign but less than two months after her offer had been accepted she stood keys in hand watching the removal van pull up with her furniture. True it did not fit with the house but there was plenty of time to replace it, all that mattered now was she was home.

It seemed strange to think that these bricks and mortar now belonged to her, but she thought of it more as a mutual thing, they belonged to each other, friends had laughed a she had tried to explain. Imogen Davis, the girl who had travelled the world living from a back pack, the least likely to put down roots had done just that, and it felt like the most normal thing in the world to her.

That weekend she invited friends round, she decided she preferred the idea of the house warming before she started searching out the furniture she pictured for each room. She spent the hours before they arrived in the kitchen. She had accumulated cook books from all round the world but never used any of them until now, she prepared a variety of foods, much to the surprise of the friends who had known her longest. This new side of her, the domestic goddess, raised eyebrows, a few took her aside double checking there was no reason for this personality change, no hidden illness or imminent arrival.

She was in her element, and by the time her friends had left, well fed and a little tipsy, they were all commenting on how well suited to the house she was. They seemed to understand why she had been drawn to it.

That night as she fell asleep she was sure she heard the house give a contented sigh as it settled down for the night.

The first sign she had that all was not quite as it seemed, was a few weeks later, when she brought home a present from work. One of the girls had been on holiday, and had brought her home a souvenir, a doll dressed in local costume, it was cheap and tacky but the thought had been there and she had not wanted to upset the girl. She brought it home and put it on the kitchen window ledge out of the way, she fully intended sticking it in a drawer, only to be brought out if the girl visited, but the phone had rung and distracted she had forgotten about it. She was only reminded when she found it in the bin as she went to throw the coffee filter in the next morning.

She was stumped, if it had fallen it would have ended up in the sink, no way could it have fallen into the bin on the other side of the kitchen. Carrying it through into the living room she dropped it on the sofa, she would figure it out after work, leaving it where it dropped, she grabbed her bag and headed out.

When she returned home she forgot all about the doll, it was only when she went to empty the bin, she found the doll once more placed there. She went round checking all the doors and windows, everywhere was locked and closed. She was at a loss to explain what had happened, was it possible that the previous owner still had a set of keys? Had he given a set to someone else and not thought to get them back?

She rung the estate agent, the brief conversation only served to add to her confusion, the previous owner had lost a set of keys after he decided to sell the house, so he had changed the locks, front and back. The two sets of keys which had been handed to her were the only ones which existed. She picked up the doll and looked at it as she shut her phone off, she took it upstairs and stuffed it in the bottom of the wardrobe. Though she checked several times over the next few days the doll stayed where it was placed.

Over the coming months she was busy, weekends spent searching second hand markets, antique shops. Every spare minute, and spare penny, she had she spent on finding the perfect furniture and decorations. The minute she walked through the door she knew immediately whether she had got it right, most of the time she had, but occasionally she would bring home an item which would be moved the same way the doll had. These items would end up in the bottom of the wardrobe until she could return them or resell them.

It was strange, these things happened but they did not scare her, she could not explain it to herself, let alone anyone else but it was like the house was her flat mate, one whose opinion she trusted. The friends who visited all talked of how welcome they felt in her house, praised the new décor as she collected it, and were happy to take the extra bits off her hands when they didn't fit in. She knew there was something, but it did not matter, she was happy, the house was happy and life was good.

The day Stuart came to work in the office she arrived with a pair of vases which the house had rejected. She walked in and dumped them on her desk, she intended to return them at lunch time, but no sooner had she put them down than Jenny from accounts wandered over, enquiring to the price tag. As always, she took a loss on them, she never liked to ask the full price from the girls at work, and as they agreed the price they joked about them not fitting in. Stuart had been stood nearby and had joined in the conversation asking if Imogen did not know what would fit with her own house before she spent money, his eye brow raised as he asked. She had blushed, she did not want to explain to this man that her house decided on the furniture, she did not need to as Jenny did it for her, but in such a way as Stuart took it as a joke.

They had lunch together several times over the next few weeks, but for some reason Imogen was reluctant to invite him out on an evening. She told herself she was taking things slowly, unsure she wanted an office romance, but as the other girls pointed out she was already having one given the number of lunches they had shared. She knew the real reason was, if they went out for an evening, then the chances were he would see her home, and then he would want to come in.

She could not decide if her main concern was that she was worried the house would not like him, or that he would not like the house, or that he would like it, but she would not want him here all the time, encroaching on her space, that she would not want to share the house. Whatever the reason was she knew she could not put it off for good.

Rather than inviting him one on one she decided the way to go was to host a dinner party, she had recently found a lovely dinner service, and as the dining table sat eight she invited everyone from the office.

Before they arrived, as she prepared the starters, she explained to the house that it would have to tolerate the doll coming out of the wardrobe, she promised it would go straight back in after but Suzanne, who had bought it, was to be amongst the guests. She did not place it in the living room though, rather she placed it on a shelf in her bedroom, she knew it would be seen as the guests took their coats up there, and they would of course, have a nosey around to see what she had done with the place.

At seven thirty the first guests arrived, she had said she would serve dinner at eight. Over the next half hour, everyone arrived, and they were relieved of coats, given a quick tour and drinks served, everyone that was except Stuart. In the kitchen as she checked on the joint roasting in the oven she spoke aloud as she sought to persuade herself that there would be a perfectly reasonable explanation.

At twenty past eight the rest of her guest took their seats, only the one remained empty. The chatter was pleasant but she could tell everyone was more than aware of the significance of the empty chair. They did their best to raise her spirits, praising the house and the delicious starter she had served, it was almost quarter past nine and they were half way through the main course when the bell rang. If she had missed the doorbell she would not have missed the pummelling her front door took as the person on the doorstep hammered on it.

She opened the door to find Stuart stood there, flowers clutched in one hand and a bottle in the other, he was giving her an excuse about a relative, and his phone battery going flat, but she could not help but notice the smell of alcohol on his breath.

She stood aside and let him in, he wandered down the corridor and into the dining room where the rest of their colleagues were eying him with suspicion. A cold breeze seemed to blow through the room as she came back through from the kitchen with the corkscrew, before realising the wine he had brought had a screw cap.

While he helped himself to the now lukewarm food, he apologised profusely, his story seeming to change slightly with each telling, something which did not go unnoticed by both Imogen and her guests. While everyone else resumed their conversations, a mixture of business and pleasure, Imogen remained quiet. She knew the house did not like him, so far it had not done anything, but she could sense it.

Suzanne was commenting on the fact she had spotted the doll she had bought her, and conversation turned to some of her recent purchases and the fact she had found it impossible to get curtains to fit the windows exactly. She was in the middle of explaining how she had come across an advert for a seamstress, circled in a newspaper she had brought home, one she picked up on the bus, when Stuart interrupted. He was laughing at her, laughing at the fact she was being so 'uptight' over curtains, why couldn't she just get them slightly bigger, no one would notice. The room went silent.

In the hallway a thud made everyone jump, Stuarts coat, which she had hung over the post at the bottom of the stairs, had been thrown against the door, as she ran to pick it up she noticed his phone had fallen from his pocket. Not only did the light screen prove he had lied about it being dead, but at that moment it rang silently, text announcing the girls name, who had evidently called numerous times according to the missed calls.

She picked up both the coat and the phone, and walked back into the room, she handed them to him, he looked confused, until he looked down at the phone. He tried to explain, but she stayed silent as she turned and left the room, seeking the refuge of the kitchen. She heard the door open and close, before Jenny came through and putting an arm round her shoulder told her they had persuaded him to leave. He had fooled them all, not just her, she was lucky to have found out what he was like before things had got serious.

Jenny joked that the house had obviously disapproved, how else could his coat have ended up where it did, Imogen did not see the humour, she knew Jenny was closer to the mark than she could ever expect.

At that moment the fridge door swung open, revealing dessert, and she could not help but smile as Jenny's eyes lit up at the sight of the triple chocolate cheesecake. No sooner did she lift it from the fridge than she felt her spirits lift, it did not matter that he had shown up and spoilt ten minutes of the evening, she had her friends, her health, and her home.

By the time everyone left she knew she would have a hangover the next morning. Standing in the kitchen alone she found herself talking to whatever it was, the spirit of the house as she thought of it, about what had happened. She had wanted it to go well, she wanted to find a special someone, okay she was not looking to settle down and get married next week, but she would like to think it was in her future, that she could find a soulmate. She even laughed as she commented that as it stood, the house was as close a soulmate as she had come to finding.

She stacked the last of the unwashed dishes in the sink, there were only a few left, she would see to them in the morning, and she would ring about the curtains. As she mounted the stairs it was as if a voice in her head was telling her to be patient, it would be okay in the end.

When she awoke next morning she headed straight to the kitchen. She went directly to the kettle, turning it on ready to make her coffee, then turning to take care of the remaining pots. Her gasp was audible as she discovered that not only had the dirty ones been washed, but all the plates and glasses had been put away, the only thing remaining in the drainer was the mug she preferred to drink her coffee from.

She had become used to small things moving over the months since she came to live here but this was the first time she had been shocked by the activity. She was not scared; she knew she had nothing to fear but all the same it made her feel faint thinking of the fact it had been able to move so many things.

She made her coffee and walked through to the living room, as it was a Sunday, normally she would not have been working, but she had agreed to go in for an hour or two to help with an audit. She drank her coffee then ran upstairs to get changed. She threw her purse and keys into her bag then looked round for her phone. It was not there.

Returning downstairs she checked in the living room, there was the phone, placed on top of the newspaper, which had been opened up on the coffee table, opened on the page showing the advert again. She picked up the phone put it in her bag and went to the door, it would not open. The phone jumped out of her bag and flew back into the room, it landed with a resolute thud back on the advert.

Imogen went to retrieve the phone again, an unknown voice sounded in her head, *call the number*, this is ridiculous she thought, but it looked like the only way she would get out of the house without further delay was to ring the number, anyway it was Sunday, chances were no one would answer.

She punched in the number, after the third ring she was about to hang up when a man answered, she explained she had seen the advert and would like to speak to the seamstress, he laughed as he explained he was the person in question. He went on to explain, he ran the business with his sister, he normally let her deal with the customers, as they seemed to feel more comfortable with a woman, especially if it required a home visit. His sister was on holiday at the minute and would be back in three weeks, he fully understood if she wanted to wait.

She hesitated, but the newspaper folding shut on the coffee table, made it clear the house was impatient. She told him what she was looking for, and arrangements were made for him to call the following evening after she got home from work, when she gave him the address he went silent. It only took him a minute to regain his cheery disposition again but when he rang off she had the distinct feeling, he knew something about the house that she didn't, and despite her asking the house was not saying either.

The day passed quickly, no one mentioned what had happened the night before, and as there were only a couple of them, and a lot of work to get through, it was easy to keep to safer subjects. She returned home and ordered a takeaway, eaten in front of the television before a bath and an earlier night. She could not help but feel the house seemed particularly cheerful, a feeling which seemed to be confirmed when she went up the stairs.

She found the doll had been stuffed back in the bottom of the wardrobe, and the flowers Stuart had brought with him, which she had just stuffed in a vase unwrapped, had been taken out of the cellophane and arranged, the vase had been placed on the ledge of the small landing window. She had to admit that though she had considered binning them they did look good there and made a mental note to keep the vase there and replace the flowers as they died.

The next morning, she went downstairs and found the kettle already on, her mug sat waiting for her next to it. As she made herself some toast she had the distinct feeling everything looked a little cleaner, a little brighter this morning, she laughed thinking it was a shame every house did not come with the spirit of a compulsive cleaner in residence.

On route to work her anxiety built at the thought of having to face Stuart on the atmosphere that would no doubt pervade the office, but her worries were not necessary. She was informed as she arrived that he had fallen down some steps on the Saturday evening after being ejected from her house, he would be off sick for the next few weeks at the very least. She did wonder if her ghost had played a part in it but dismissed the idea from her head, after all, whatever she shared her house with was tied to the house. It could not have followed him and besides the spirit had been there, opening the fridge door, and cleaning up after she went to bed. By she could not shake off the feeling that there was more to his accident than a simple fall.

She got stuck in traffic in the way home and as she pulled up she noticed the tall blonde man stood at her door with an armful of fabric samples. She could understand immediately why he left the face to face stuff to his sister, he was tall and broad, the parts of his arms she could see between his rolled up shirt sleeves and the material he carried showed tattoos. He looked more like a boxer than a seamstress.

As she stepped out of the car he turned to greet her, his smile was warm and genuine, he reached out his hand to shake hers as he introduced himself almost dropping the samples in the process. She felt at ease with him straight away, and as they stepped into the house she had a feeling the house liked him as well.

They were in the living room, the seamstress, Dave, was laying out samples while explaining he did not need to take the actual measurements. They already had the sizes for each window on file, he was telling her about the fabrics the previous owner had chosen. She felt there was something he was holding back on, and she felt the house still as if it were waiting for a revelation. Then it came.

He was telling her what a terrible tragedy it had been, how lovely the girl who lived here had been, he had only met her once when he came with his sister to fit the curtains. She had been so sweet, but her boyfriend, well he had been a real arse, stuck up, spoke to them, and her for that matter like dirt. She found herself opening up to this man in return about the house, her love life or lack of it.

She thought afterward, that she would not have been surprised had he decided to run a mile, but instead he told her about his life, his failed marriage, and they found three hours had passed in conversation before realising she has still not decided on a single fabric. When he suggested leaving them so she could sleep on it, and he would collect them the following evening, she jumped at the offer, maybe, he suggested they could go out for a drink when he picked them up.

He had not given her the details of what had happened to the girl who lived here, he had carefully evaded the actual facts. After he left she went upstairs to the smaller bedroom that she was in the process of making into an office, she had come up with a possible solution, she turned on the computer and opened a word document.

She knew the spirit, ghost, whatever it was, had the power to move things, so now she began typing pausing at the end of each question, to allow the response to appear.

What is your name?

Hannah Louise Smith.

Did you live here?

You know the answer to that, yes, I lived here, and I died here, but I like you living here. I think we could have been friends in life, I would like us to be friends now, because I am not going anywhere and I don't want you to either. You were the only one who came to view the house that I liked.

How did you die?

I like the pale blue material with the tiny flowers on for the landing window.

How did you die?

What about the cornflower blue but with a gingham trim for the downstairs windows?

No gingham, and will you answer the question, how did you die?...

I'm waiting, how did you die, just answer…

Okay, I killed myself, I slit my wrists in the middle of the living room, happy now?

No, but why, why did you do it?

Because I was losing everything, I had no family, he had driven away most of my friends, then he found someone else and was taking away my home. This was his house, but I made it a home, I spent houses on it not to mention all my savings, I was creating the perfect home for the children we were going to have for the life we were going to have together, then he told me, it wasn't what he wanted, I wasn't what he wanted. He was going to move her in here, so I forced him into a position where he would have to sell it, he would have to pay me back for the work I put into it and the value my work had added, I knew he would have to sell he had no savings of his own, he enjoyed spending too much.

Why didn't you buy him out?

He wouldn't give me the time I needed to get the money together, then I discovered his plan with his parents, they were going to buy the house off him for just enough to pay me off but he would go on living here, he would get the property back later, I was not having that.

So you killed yourself?

I know it seems crazy now, but it made sense at the time. I had nothing left to live for, or that was how I felt, and if I did it here, did it in the house, well he would never want to live here again, or that was what I thought.

You mean he wanted to live here still? What happened?

Well, it didn't take long to get rid of them, he moved her in, they spent a week trying to pretend nothing was happening, and it took some practise to be able to move the bigger things, but once actual furniture started moving, they could not really ignore me anymore. Actually I felt sorry for her, turned out she never knew I existed in the first place. Are you sure about the gingham? It would look really cute in the kitchen.

Yes, I am sure, it might look cute in the kitchen but hideous in the living room and I want all the curtains to match. I can't believe I am arguing with a ghost over curtains, if we are going to share this house we need rules but I am tired right now, we will work them out later okay?

Okay, I am glad you came to live here, can I ask a favour, can we leave this on? It will be a lot easier for me to be able to leave you messages on here than moving things about, hoping you get the hint.

Okay, night.

Night.

Imogen stood up and headed to her own room, as she did she looked around at the house, she could not imagine ever leaving here, the idea of being forced to, she wondered would she have done the same as Hannah? No, she could not have done it, but she did understand, she could see how a person in pain and fear might act that way. Living with a dead housemate was going to take some getting used to, it was different now she knew who it was, and she wondered how they would both adapt, she supposed the house rules would be more or less the same as if they had both been living.

As she climbed into bed she noticed her clothes moving from where she had dropped them on the floor into the washing basket, *rule number one*, she called out, *will be my bedroom is off limits*. She heard a laugh, then turned out the light and went to sleep.

Downstairs, the contented ghost of Hannah was looking at fabric samples, she hated to admit it but Imogen was right about the gingham.

THE LIBRARY

The woman climbed the steps of the large stone building. Its small numerous windows looked down on her, like a thousand small eyes. They seemed to follow her progress towards the heavy, wooden doors. She opened them and passed through into the open foyer.

Brightly lit and spacious, a large staircase rose directly in front of her, the sign on the landing directing visitors to the reference library on the floor above. She turned her attention to her right and moved towards the door situated there, the words 'Lending Library' were chiselled into the stone mantel, and hoisting the books she carried to shift the weight a little, she entered.

She placed the pile of books she was returning in front of the librarian, who was so engrossed in arranging a tray of index cards she barely even noticed anything else around her. Freed from her cumbersome load she headed off into the labyrinth of bookshelves. As in all libraries the shelves were divided into sections, she felt comfortable here among the books, if she could she would happily move in here. She smiled at the idea of pitching a tent down a lesser used aisle and wondered how long it would take someone to discover her.

She allowed her hand to run along the shelves, caressing the spines of the books, as her fingertips brushed the mixture of card, paper and leather. She longed to pull out individual volumes for closer inspection, but resisted, knowing if she began to let her mind wander she would be here all day, and as much as she would love that, the time was a luxury she did not have. She passed down familiar aisles 'Biography", 'Historical Fiction'. She moved without thought towards her destination; 'Science Fiction.'

Suddenly she felt a cold breeze across the back of her neck. She stopped. The hairs on the back of her neck now standing, she turned and gazed into the empty aisle. She looked round for an air vent; anything to explain the breeze. There was nothing.

She gave herself a little shake. *This is stupid*! She took another step, there it was again, and again with the next step!

She stopped.

She could feel someone, behind her, breathing on her neck. There was a strange smell, faded perfume, floral and sweet. Again she spun round to confront the person she expected to be there; she found no one, just and empty space. For a moment she was disorientated; not sure what to do. She wanted to run but remained there rooted to the spot. Then she noticed the section she stood in 'Ghost Stories & Supernatural.'

She let out a nervous laugh, *I don't believe in ghosts,* but she still glanced over her shoulder before she turned her focus back to her errand. She tried to get her bearings straight, she was sure she must have taken a wrong turn, everything seemed to be in the wrong place. The shelves before her now holding a selection of ghost stories had been gardening on her last visit, but it seemed impossible they would shuffle the whole library in a few days, it would take longer than that surely.

She decided to steer towards the back corner where she expected to find her favourite romance novels, they were her escape from the confines of her everyday life. Though she was not sure she held out any hope of her knight in shining armour appearing to save her, the fantasy that it might be possible was how she found the strength to get through each day. Between the romances, and the adventures in space, or travel through time, she managed to shut out real life.

She shook her head, like a dog throwing off water, reality returned but the feeling she was not alone persisted. A noise startled her, a dropped book perhaps? She turned on the spot, maybe if she was quick enough she would catch a glimpse of the culprit over her shoulder before they had chance to disappear. If she could just move quickly enough, but nothing, then the sight of a book returning, sliding into the shelf, sent her into a tail spin.

Frantically she fled between the shelves, books flying through the air in her wake, her fear and panic increasing with each step, she could not understand why no one came to her rescue, or to investigate the commotion.

Several times she felt something brush against her, the skimming of fingertips against her skin, the blast of warm breath on her cheek. Some invisible creature stalked her, but no, surely there was more than one. Each turn she made left her assaulted by more sensations, her hair caught as if someone had grabbed for it but caught only a few wisps, her clothes snagged against unseen obstacles. Her panic increased, driving her on faster and more frantically until she lost all sense of the direction she travelled in.

Finally she found herself in a corner, frightened and trapped, the shelves closed in on her. Ripping her nails she scrabbled at the wooden shelves as if she could claw her way through them, searching for a way to find salvation before slumping, cowering to the ground. Defeated, she curled up in a ball, arms wrapped tightly round her head, desperately trying to fend off the expected blows.

She sat waiting.

Then everything around her stilled, she peeped out from between her shielding arms and looked around her. The hairs stood on her arms, a random memory came back to her of the static from balloons rubbed against her jumper as a child. Inhaling deeply she noticed the smell of perfume again, this one was strong, musk possibly, Jasmine perhaps, it made her think of the days she had walked round department stores, walking past the counters where the woman stood misting the air to lure shoppers in.

Her fear was subsiding and she found herself becoming calmer, she knew she had wasted precious time, she should probably leave now, but she could not bear the idea of leaving empty handed. She turned searching to trace her normal path between the shelves, searching for the titles she desired.

She turned a corner, and stood before her was a man, a shiver passed through her and she mentally scolded herself for her foolishness but that did not stop her flinching and preparing to retrace her steps as he turned towards her. It was his smile that stopped her, *sunshine and daisies*, the image flashed through her mind, simpler times when she had smiled in the same way.

"It's okay. You don't have to go, Can I help you?"

She could not help but think his voice matched his smile, harsh words could never spill forth from that soft mouth, but such thoughts were foolish, and lies, she had learnt that from experience,

"No, everything is fine, sorry to have disturbed you." She backed away but her shaking was visible.

"You don't have to be scared, no one is going to hurt you. You are safe here."

"No! No! I'm not, I'm not safe anywhere, I never will be."

As the woman spoke these last words she flickered and disappeared. The man shook his head sadly and replaced the book he was holding.

He looked round searching out a staff member, there was a young girl sorting out the returned books ready to replace them on the shelves, she jumped at the man's approach.

"Can you tell me about the ghost?"

She stood frozen, a book clutched in mid-air, as if she had forgotten where it needed to go before it slipped from her hand and landed with a thud upside down on the carpet. Either the noise or the motion animated her, and she swooped down to pick it up before turning to face him.

"She was a member here, she came once a week every week and stayed for exactly forty-five minutes, never a minute over. She was quiet and kept herself to herself, I know lots of us tried to befriend her, but she always kept us at arm's length."

"Did you ever guess why?"

"She tried to cover the bruises, most of the time, I guess they were in places where they couldn't be seen. The signs were there though, the long sleeves and jumpers in Summer, glimpses of purple on her wrists as she reached for a book, the slip of a scarf showing hand prints on her neck. We wanted to help her, but what could we do if she wouldn't let us?

She looked imploringly at the man, searching his face for a sign of understanding. He nodded giving her the encouragement to continue.

"One day she came in, she seemed more nervous than normal, she had a routine, it was almost a ritual. You could have set your clock by her movements, return books, Science section first, she didn't always take books out from there, maybe only once a month but she spent the longest time there browsing, on to Sci-Fi then to Romance, always the same routine, always the same amount of time spent in each section."

"Was something different that day? Did she say something?"

"No, she didn't say anything, if only she had… that day she dropped her books off but instead of stopping to look at the new books she rushed straight off to the Romance section. We noticed the man come in, but we had no idea who he was. If we had known we could have warned her, hidden her somewhere maybe, or found a way to get her out. But maybe if we had, if we had found a way to help her that day it would have only have delayed what happened."

"I know this is hard but I promise you I'm not just asking for the sake of it."

"It happened quickly, he was screaming at her, accusing her of meeting someone, another man. He was shouting that the books were just a cover, telling her she was too stupid to be reading the books she brought home.

That was a lie, she never met anyone else and she was smart, I remember once commenting about one of the science books as she checked it out, and I said how it was beyond my understanding. She let it slip that she had studied physics at university, but no sooner had she began telling me she went silent again, but for that brief second I swear I saw her come alive, truly alive for the first time."

"Did she say where she studied?"

"No, nothing. Anyway, one of the other clerks had called for the police but it was too late, he had her by the hair and he was dragging her up and down the aisles looking for this imaginary man she was supposed to be meeting. We were shouting at him but the more we shouted, the angrier he got, so, we went quiet, thinking he might stop then but he didn't.

I guess he was frustrated that he had been proved wrong, maybe he blamed her for the fact we were all looking at him like he was dirt. Next thing we knew he threw her against a bookshelf, then he flew at her, he was punching her and kicking her. She went down on the floor and he kept going, there was so much blood, it was everywhere. I couldn't just watch. I ran over and started throwing books at him, for a second I thought he was going to come after me, he looked at me and I saw evil stare back at me, then he just turned back and carried on. By then I could tell by the way she was laying and how much blood there was that it didn't matter anymore, no one could save her."

Tears were flowing down the girls face as she finished telling her story and the man reached out and placed a hand on her shoulder, at his touch she looked up searching his face.

"How did you know? Sometimes I think I see her but I can never be sure, I hoped she had gone, I would hate to think of her trapped here. Please, please tell me she won't be having to keep going through it?"

"I think at the minute she does, but I saw her and she saw me. I can help her if she lets me, and if you will allow me to come back tonight after closing time."

"It's not up to me, but give me a minute and I will get you someone who can arrange it."

The girl walked over to an older woman and began talking animatedly, gesturing backwards towards the man who stood watching the exchange. He was confused by the expressions passing over the older woman's face, there was concern but also something he could not quite put his finger on.

She looked stern, every bit the librarian capable of silencing a room with a glance, and although she was doing her best to keep her emotions hidden, he could see contempt flit across her lips. She strode towards him, the business like attitude and determination showing a strength one would not have expected from her frail frame.

"What do you actually want to do? I know she is here; I haven't seen her myself, though I know others have, but I will not have any silly business going on in my library that will risk bringing more trouble here."

She waited for his response, arms crossed in front of her and a severe look on her face, the man could not help but think she would be a match for the majority of the dead as well as the living.

"I only want to talk to her, I am not going to do anything else, no Ouija boards, no calling forth other spirits, I just want to talk to her. I want to make sure she understands what happened, give her a choice, let her go into the light or stay, but I want to help her so that if she wants to stay she stays here safely, not reliving the end. Right now she looks scared, she looks haunted."

"How can a ghost look haunted? Please do not give me a sob story young man. I was not here when it happened but, I have heard it all, and I have seen the police reports, I really cannot imagine why she would want to stay here given what happened. But never the less, when we close at eight I shall allow you thirty minutes, while we finish tidying up you can try to talk with her, once we are finished so are you, understood?"

"Yes, thank you."

He wanted to say more but she was already moving back to her previous task, the girl looked across at him and smiled, relief evident in her face. She had obviously expected her colleague to refuse his request.

As the local clock tower struck eight he heard the bolts being drawn across the heavy outer door. He moved back through the aisles to where he had seen the woman earlier. In the time he had been waiting for the library to close he had not been idle, he had done his research and now pulled a slip of paper from his pocket bearing the dead woman's name.

He was about to begin calling out to her when he realised he was not alone; the girl was watching him furtively from round the end of a book shelf.

"You want to help?"

"Yes, no, I mean I do but I can't, I need to get these books put back but if she comes, if she talks to you, please tell her I'm sorry. I should have done something else, acted quicker, just tell her I am sorry please."

"Stay and tell her yourself, look this won't take long if she does decide to talk, and if she doesn't want to, it will be over even quicker. Come here and give me your hands, you don't need to do anything other than think about the woman's face."

He took her hands then closed his eyes, he focused on the name that was written on the paper still held in his hand, he repeated it over and over again.

She felt herself flying through the air, she was being pulled to the library, conscious that she was not moving of her own volition but at someone else's, then as abruptly as the move had begun, she came to a halt in front of two figures.

The man and the girl were still holding hands, they almost looked like a couple at the altar taking vows and she could not suppress the giggle before it slipped from her lips. Instantly she clamped her hand over her mouth just as two pairs of eyes flew open and turned to look at her.

"Hello. Thank you for coming, I just want to talk to you and help if I can."

"Hello again. I really had no choice in coming, I think you know that. And as for helping me, well I think it is a little late for that, don't you?"

It was the girl who spoke up next, her voice trembled as she struggled to control her emotions.

"I'm sorry, I'm so sorry, I tried, I really did, but, I should… I should have…"

The woman held up a hand as she interrupted her.

"You have nothing to apologise for. I know you tried to help, so many did over the years, but there really was nothing you could have done. I always knew it would end that way, it was inevitable really. We all make choices we have to live with, or die with, but in the end we are only responsible for ourselves. You can never really save anyone else, they have to be willing to save themselves."

"You know what happened then? You know you are dead? Then why are you still here? Why don't you move on? When I saw you before you were reliving it, you didn't know you were dead then, I know you didn't, so how do you know now?"

It was the man firing questions at her, rapid fire finding it's mark and leaving a sad smile upon her lips.

"Because it is not that simple. Yes, I know what happened and that I died. I am here because I saw the light but I was too scared to go and then it was too late, the light was gone. I visit like this, in full knowledge of the end when I can, because this was my haven, my refuge but the price is sometimes I have to relive it, there is always a price to pay…"

"Why? Why didn't you leave him? Why didn't you let us help you? You knew we would have, don't you? We could have got you somewhere safe, if we had known who he was we would have hidden you that day, we would have found a way to protect you."

"Sweet girl, you could not have protected me anymore than I could have run from him. Oh don't get me wrong, I tried, I tried several times but when the person you are running from is rich and powerful, your options are somewhat limited. I went to refuges, safe houses, but he always found me, and when he did, well things would always get worse.

You have to understand we were both good at hiding things. Everyone thought he was the perfect husband, so attentive and caring, maybe a little over protective, that is irony isn't it? The only person I ever needed him to protect me from was himself, and he could never see that what he was doing was wrong."

She paused now, as if reflecting on her own words, the sadness that radiated from her was palpable, when she continued she addressed her answers to the man.

"You ask why I didn't go into the light? I was scared but the real answer is simple, I needed to be sure no one else got hurt, it didn't matter what he did to me, that was my choice, no I don't mean that, but he was my choice, but this girl and the others who tried to help? No, I could not allow him to hurt them, I have no idea what I could have done if it had come to it but I still needed to be sure."

They were interrupted by the older woman's appearance from behind a bookshelf, she stopped in front of them, arms crossed, staring at the man.

"I thought the idea was you would help this young woman, not just question her for your own amusement. Now can you help her or not? Or are you hoping if you talk at her for long enough she will disappear through boredom?"

It was apparent the older woman could neither see nor hear the ghost, the man nodded then turned his attention back to the spirit, who was looking at the librarian with a warm smile.

"You say the light went away? Do you want my help? Do you want to move on?"

"I don't know. I am scared, I have no idea what is waiting there, he killed himself in prison, or so I heard, will he be there? If I do go, can I come back?" Can I still come back and visit the library? It gave me the only little bit of pleasure I had over the last few years."

"I can't be sure but I think you will be able to come back and visit if you want to, but I have a feeling once you pass over and go into the light you probably won't want to come back, you won't need to. I can't make you go; it is your choice."

She nodded and appeared to be considering her options, the man noticed she was looking at the librarian again before she fixed him with a resolute gaze.

"I want to go, it is time."

The man bowed his head acknowledging her decision before beginning to recite a verse. It flowed from his lips flawlessly, obviously well-rehearsed, calling forth the light and the woman's loved ones to step forward and guide her in her passage.

At first nothing happened, then slowly a ball of bright white light began to form, as it reached the size of a golf ball he increased the vigour of his recitation, he kept it up until it was the size of a normal doorway and the spirit stood framed by its brilliance.

Even the librarian could see her now and they stood and stared transfixed by the beauty of the light in which the woman was bathed as she gave them a final smile. She seemed to be taking a last look around the bookshelves before turning and taking a final step into the light beyond their field of vision.

The light shrank immediately to a pinprick, flaring once before it disappeared completely, leaving the three of them standing staring at an empty space.

When the man turned he noticed tears in the eyes of both women, and was shocked to see that it was the older woman who seemed most upset. As soon as she realised his gaze was upon her, the mask slid back into place, and she gave the appearance of having regained her composure.

"Well, now you have sent my daughter to the other side, and distracted my assistant, maybe you can help put those books back so we can all get home tonight."

Without looking at them she strode away down an aisle, leaving the man and the girl staring after her.

The House

The girl dropped to her knees. She reached out to brush her hand against the lush, green grass, then recoiled in anguish. Her hand passed through the blades, a slight tingling sensation all she could feel in her fingertips. She turned her gaze to the house, the whitewash looked faded, paint flaked slightly around the windows. The lawns and hedges, it was still tidy, but did not quite live up to the exact standards she remembered. It was as though several storms had passed without the careful repairs taking place in between to put everything back exactly as it should be.

Out of the corner of her eye she caught sight of the orchard to the left of the house, apples which should have been picked and stored weeks ago lay strewn across the grass beneath the trees, spoiled and decayed. Cook would be furious at the waste.

Memories flooded back to her, she recalled happy times here, not always, that she was painfully aware of, but at this moment it was the laughter she remembered. She could hear the echoes of the gaiety drift towards her as she sat and looked up at the imposing, white building before her.

She closed her eyes and could almost smell the food the cook prepared in the kitchen, grand sumptuous meals, not for their consumption, but for the ladies and gentlemen who would have descended from their carriages onto the gravel which formed the border between the house and lawn. She had waited with the others, secretly hoping for leftovers to be returned from the dining room, even though they knew when that happened it would put cook in a foul mood and they would suffer in other ways.

It had been a hard life, but she knew compared to some she had been lucky, of course at the time she had known no different, life was simply life. Their mistress had not been kind but nor had she been particularly harsh, rather she treated her servants and slaves the way one would treat unruly children, punishment was doled out to those who earned it. The master left those who worked in the house to his wife's control, something she had been grateful for, she had heard the stories of his discipline whispered about in the slave quarters.

She doubted the master or even the mistress had ever noticed her existence any more than they had noticed the chickens in the yard. She had been taught to be invisible, that those who provided her daily bread should never have to look upon her face, and, that if they ever had reason to, she would have been lucky had she lived to regret it. She shuddered at the thought of the warnings the cook had given her and the other young girls who worked in the kitchen and the yard, she had always don't her best to obey, to be a good girl.

She rose to her feet slowly, aware her feet did not really touch the ground, rather she walked as if a thin layer of water lay between the soles of her feet and the grass over which she travelled. She began to move towards the house, drawn onwards by something she did not understand. She only knew she had to find the answers. Answers to questions she wasn't sure of. She only knew somewhere deep inside that when she found the answers everything would be alright.

She approached the house, nervous that she would be seen near the front entrance, she knew her place and it was not here. She stood at the bottom of the steps that led up to the wrap around porch, some sort of swinging bench sat to the right, she was sure it had not been there before. She tried to remember what the house had looked like before from here, only to realise she would not have known, she would never have been at the front and even in the orchard her eyes would have remained firmly on the ground unless commanded elsewhere.

She could hear the sound of children's laughter from beyond the door. Like her vision, the sounds she heard had a surreal quality, each had an almost musical tone. She crept up the stairs fearful of being caught and whipped for being found here. She felt she should turn away and go round the side of the house to the rear, the thoughts there even though she knew she was in no danger. There came laughter again, like a peal of bells rippling through the air, curiosity drove her on, the master and mistress had never had children, well not ones that had lived, the only children who had been here had been like her, slaves born and bred.

She reached for the door handle instinctively.

She knew she had been away, it had been lovely and warm there, like being wrapped in a huge fluffy blanket. She had slept, and dreams she would never have believed she could create, had filled her mind. She had been safe and at peace. The she had awakened to find herself back here, her first sensation being that of the grass beneath her feet, but maybe she hadn't, maybe this was just another dream.

She reached out once more and attempted to grasp the handle again, the tingle, as her hand passed through it for a second time. There was only one thing for it, she took a deep breath and stepped into the door. The sensation passed through her entire body; inside the hallway she paused listening for the laughter which had drawn her in, but she could no longer hear it.

She could tell a great deal had changed here as well, not that she had seen a much of this part of the house; the servant's quarters were round the back. That was the direction she moved in now, curiously peering into the rooms as she passed. The sitting room, where the high backed chairs and settees had been replaced with large, soft looking seats, clustered around a large black box with pictures flickering on it.

She stopped for a moment transfixed by the images, the laughter was coming from the box. Tiny children ran around playing inside it, like a living doll's house, they were seemingly trapped but happy to be so. She felt the air move as a strange man walked by her, picked up a black oblong from the table, and pointed it at the box, the pictures changed as he sank into one of the chairs.

She moved on again, past the dining room, that at least, still looked familiar with its colonial grandeur. The sixteen seat dining table was still the same one she had spent many hours rubbing wax into, scrubbing so hard until her reflection had shone back at her from the glass like finish. She had only seen the table fully laid once, when she was sent up with a spoon that had been left behind after polishing. She had received a smack to the side of her head from the footman, all for another's mistake, but it had been worth it just to marvel at the sight she had seen. The glass and silver had sparkled in the candlelight, like a million stars brought down from the sky, and the smell from the huge floral centrepiece had continued to fill her nostrils long after she had returned downstairs.

She closed her eyes, the scent of lilies and roses transporting her back through time for a moment, and a smile formed on her lips at the remembrance of details she had allowed to fade. When she opened her eyes again the myriad of tiny differences between the room of her memory and the one she stood in became apparent. They had been so subtle she had not noticed at first, the candles in the chandelier no longer held flickering flames, there were no rivulets of wax to worry about dropping down, now each branch held a solid stem of illumination, every jewelled branch evenly lit. The plates in the cabinet are not the gilded cream porcelain, so fine and delicate when you held them up the light glowed through them, but in their place is a gaudy red and black set, decorated with a geometric pattern.

She left the room and continue, torn between the desire to explore and the need for answers which pulled her here. At the end of the corridor she paused, composed herself, then passed through the door to the kitchen and servants quarters.

For a moment she was confused, the room she stood in bore no resemblance to the kitchen she knew. The wood burning stove and open fireplace that had dominated the far wall was gone. The larder, the pantry and the cool store all gone, making the room larger and brighter. The dark wood shelves and worktops also gone, replaced by a sea of shiny metal. She noticed how cool it seemed; looking up she expected to see the large ceiling fan, but that too was gone. Bright shining pans hung from a rack above a central work table, she looked round for the heavy black cast iron pans she had spent hours scrubbing clean, the only ones she could see stood with plants growing from them, decorative rather than functional.

The big trough sinks, where the lowest of the kitchen maids had spent hours with hands submerged in water straight from the kettle, which had boiled constantly on the fireplace, were gone. In their place, small sparkling silver bowls, that would have struggled to hold even the servant's pots, let alone the those used by the master, family and guests. Huge glass doors opened out onto the garden beyond, tables and chairs standing on the flagstones where the chickens had wandered and she, alongside others, had pumped water from the well that now stood overflowing with flowers cascading down its sides.

So much changed, so much she could not understand! She felt so lost, lonely, why was she here? Why now, when so much time had passed?

The door to the servant's quarters stood before her. She wondered what to expect when she passed through, would the rooms still be there, or like the rest of the house would they have changed?

They had been small, cramped, dark, damp rooms, where she had spent the time when she wasn't scrubbing or heaving buckets of water from the river to fill the wash tubs. The pump outside had only been used for water for the kitchen. For washing she had struggled the mile or so up from the river bank, heavy skins sloshing against her back, the weight pressing her, making her lean forward. Every day she had made that journey at least once, sometimes if she had been disobedient she was sent a second or third time, but she was out in the open air, compared to other punishments it had been a blessing, hurting only her flesh but not her soul.

She knew she had to pass through, the answers she needed were on the other side of that door. She stood frozen to the spot, torn between the urge to go on and fear of what awaited her there. A noise on the other side of the door startled her into action; before she had time to think about what she was doing she was through. Before her was a larger space than she had expected, some of the walls had already been knocked down, piles of bricks scattered around.

In one corner two men sat eating sandwiches, she stood and watched as they finished off their lunch. She had the feeling she must wait for something to happen, she didn't know what, but her entire body was awash with the anticipation.

The men rose from their seats and picked up the heavy hammers resting against the wall. Her memory told her there had been two small rooms at the far end of the space she now stood in, one had been used for storing coal, the other, she shivered as she thought it, the room used to punish her for the slightest digression.

There behind the remaining wall, the tiny chamber stood still intact. It had been dark, and so cold at night, but like an oven during the day when the sun flooded the chamber from the window set high in the wall. The window had been sealed shut, not the slightest breeze had infiltrated the stale air. Alone she would curl up on the floor, hard compacted dirt, offering no comfort as she waited to see how long her punishment would last. Sometimes it would be an hour, other times it would last until the next day. In part the length of the punishment was determined by the crime, in part by how busy they were and whether she could be of use at the time.

She tried to remember the reasons she had been sent here, what terrible transgression she had committed to be condemned on this occasion but she could not be sure there really was one.

She had the impression the master and his family had been away from home, she was sure had he been there they would have been too busy to have left her there for long. She had a vague recollection of one of the other maids taunting her, saying one of the field slaves had whistled at her as they had come back from the river that morning. Her face screwed up, a frown appearing on her forehead, could she really have been punished for someone whistling at her, something she had no control over, something that meant nothing to her?

She knew the answer was of course yes, but thought it more likely she had answered back at the allegations. It was far more likely the whistles had been aimed at the kitchen maid who had been with her, she had been a little older, and had recently developed curves, with which had come increased attention and respect from the male servants and more scolding's from the cook.

She watched as the men lifted the hammers, poised to strike at the wall. It seemed there was a pause, when even time held its breath, before the arc of the hammer falling towards its target commenced. As contact was made memories assaulted her.

She was no longer stood outside watching the hammer fall, she was back in the room, trapped and alone. No room to move, begging to be let out, screaming and crying. She couldn't breathe, her hands flew to her throat, they knew, they knew how scared she was, but they stood, stood and laughed while she screamed.

The door had swung wide briefly, taunting her with escape but as she tried to dash forth, she had been grabbed by rough hands and thrown back unceremoniously to the ground. The kitchen maid had stood over her, hands on her hips as she taunted her. Behind her two of the male house slaves, they cared nothing for her, they were only interested in trying to gain favour with the young woman whose curves had become weapons in the battle for position within the ranks of the oppressed. She could not understand how this woman had changed in such a short time from the girl she had clung to in fear during the night hours, when the footsteps had paused outside their room.

The darkness had enclosed her again with the slamming home of the bolt. The sun had already passed by the window on its daily travels, and the last vestiges of warmth had dissipated. Crawling into the corner she had sought to disappear, her breathing ragged, the shallow gasps barely inflating her chest becoming faster.

Then a different type of darkness and the feeling of falling through, through what? Like air? No, that was not the right description, there was no breeze, but not like water either, she strained to grasp at the feeling.

Then as suddenly as the memories had come, they were gone. She focused once again on the men and their hammers smashing the wall down, one stopped and cried out. His workmate downed tools and joined him looking at the floor just out of her sight. She knew she had to look. There beyond the wall was her answer. All she had to do was step forward, it seemed like time had stopped as she moved in the direction of the men's gaze.

Then she saw and understood.

Her hand reached out towards the bones lying on the floor, she had never left there. She remembered huddling in the corner, praying for release that had never come. She recalled how tired she had felt, she had welcomed the sleep that had overtaken her, the weight of her eyelids had become more than she could bare and she had surrendered to the dark.

As she made contact with the skeleton, she felt a sense of peace sweep over her.

The world around her shimmered and faded. She became aware of a light, warm and inviting, and she knew it was time to go, to let go of the past.

THE COTTAGE

Rachel picked up the canvas and flung it across the room. *Useless*! Nothing she had produced for weeks had satisfied her. It was all his fault. Ever since she had caught him in a compromising position with his life model, the one he had persuaded her to hire, her eyes saw only that image. It was as if it were burnt into her retinas.

Today she had been working on a still life, it should have been simple, nothing to disturb her. Yet, as she focused on the petals of the flowers, they had transformed before her eyes into twisted human limbs, encircling each other, entwined, so caught up in their own passion they had not observed her as she had stood in the doorway.

She threw her paintbrush at the floral arrangement, it bounced off, its failure to inflict damage mocking her. Her feelings of inadequacy boiled within her as she looked round for another missile. Her palette connected with the vase but lacked the weight to dislodge it, it wobbled on the stand before resuming its position, the only sign of upset, the thin trickle of water racing down the vase, mirroring the one on her cheek.

She needed to get away, go somewhere else, to escape her own life and more importantly her memories. The phone rang, she picked it up and checked the caller ID before she answered.

"Rachel? Sis, are you there?"

"Yes, I'm here, where else would I be?"

"Well… that is the exact reason I am calling. You could be in an idyllic country retreat, miles from anywhere. A friend of mine is selling a cottage she just inherited from an aunt, or some other relative she didn't know she had. I wasn't really paying attention until she mentioned she could do with someone to go down there and straighten the place up. You know the sort of thing, eyes on the ground, or somewhere, but basically someone she can trust to give her the low down on the state of things and show potential buyers round, that sort of thing. She doesn't want to go down herself, and doesn't want to have to trust strangers to deal with everything, not when she doesn't know what there is there herself. So are you interested?"

"Why would I want to go to the middle of nowhere and sit in someone else's empty house?"

There was silence on the other end of the phone and Rachel imagined her sisters' face, pained on her behalf, they both knew exactly why she wanted to get away and that she needed somewhere to go,

"She is actually willing to pay for a house sitter, the money will come in useful…" Her sister's voice trailed off conscious she had unwittingly rubbed salt in to the wounds by alluding to the fact that Rachel's douchebag ex owned the flat, even though it had been Rachel's earnings that paid the bills and the mortgage. Rachel had not only had her heart broken but now would also have to vacate the home she loved.

"I'll do it. Email me the details and her number, I'll arrange to move my stuff into storage before I go. May as well make it a fresh start, nothing left for me here."

The last words were little more than a whisper as she replaced the handset.

It was a week later and the time had flown past surprisingly quickly, she had arranged for her furniture to go into storage until she returned, if she decided to return to the area. It was only as she began to select the pieces that were hers to take, she realised how much of the flat was hers, he may have owned the bricks and mortar but everything that made it a home was down to her.

Some things she could not take, the deluxe bathroom suite she had paid for, she considered taking a hammer to it; the huge wooden four poster bed she left because no matter how many clean sheets she put on it, it would always be the site of her betrayal, silly as it seemed, she almost felt like it had conspired with them.

She considered being spiteful, removing the blinds and curtains she had handmade to fit the awkwardly shaped windows, but she lacked the energy to tear them down, tempting as it was. She had put in to take a six month unpaid leave of absence from her job so she had to also be realistic about the size of storage unit she could afford, her sister had suggested she just sell everything, and she probably would, but for now she could not face it.

As she gathered up the last few bits to take with her, things that had no bitter memories associated with them, she recalled the long hours she had put in working for an advertising agency, putting her own painting on a back burner to support them both so he could be freed from financial woes to concentrate on his art, *maybe if he had put the same amount of concentration into painting his model as screwing her he might have been more successful.*

The real irony had been, though she would never have said it herself, that she was the better painter, but, he had persuaded her that it was his passion, that he needed it more, told her she was his muse and she had been flattered. She had loved him completely.

She had packed her painting gear and enough clothes to last a few weeks into the two large suitcases that now sat beside her on the pavement. The taxi pulled away and she stood taking in the view.

The cottage could have been taken straight from the lid of a box of chocolates, in fact the longer she stared, the more convinced she became that it was the same cottage that had featured on the chocolates she remembered having pride of place on the dresser at their grandmothers house. She made a note to research it later, assuming she could connect to the internet.

Roses climbed round the doorway, their crimson blooms contrasted against the ivy that enveloped the rest of the building. Lead paned windows peeked out from the foliage and she wondered how much light they would actually let into the rooms.

One at a time, she half carried, half dragged, the suitcases down the garden path to the door. She slid a hand into her pocket and pulled out the envelope containing the keys. It had been arranged that the estate agent would meet her here at the cottage, but during her journey down on the train she had received a text message, informing her of a change of plans, which had resulted in the keys being left in the station office for her collection.

The station itself had provided what could only be described as a culture shock. The shuttle train had seemed bizarrely out of place as it had pulled into the old fashioned station. She could not remember the last time she had seen such an abundance of planters, hanging baskets and bunting. She had actually wondered if someone special had been expected.

The station master had rushed forward, eager to assist her and see her safely loaded into a taxi, the keys transferred into her possession. As they pulled away from the station she noticed there was no sign of a taxi rank, and the car park only had space for two or three cars at most, she made a mental note to thank the estate agent for arranging for one to be there waiting to collect her.

As she thought about it now, removing the key from its paper prison, she had been the only person to alight from the train, maybe that explained why the guard had been so happy to help, anything to break up the boredom, it had been a change from the brusque guards she was used to in the city stations,

She looked down at the bunch of keys, there were half a dozen, of various sizes and shapes, she glanced up at the lock then back at the keys, she narrowed it down to two possible choices. The second caused the door to swing open. She stood peering into the darkness for a moment before instinctively ducking down and passing under the low mantel and into the cottage.

It took a few minutes for her eyes to adjust to the dim light, as she feared, the overgrown foliage had reduced the amount of natural light the windows let in. She would have to enquire in the village for a gardener who could come cut them back a little. As she looked round she shivered as she recollected that everything in this house belonged to a woman who was recently deceased. The furnishings and ornaments all screamed country kitchen, she smiled as she corrected herself, they screamed cliché country cottage, it was almost like a TV set for a period drama, she could not believe that places like this still existed in real life.

An inspection of the upper level confirmed her worst fear, there was only one bedroom. It was situated at the top of a steep flight of stairs, going up it was more like climbing a ladder than a staircase and she wondered how an old lady had managed living here. Nestled beneath the sloping roof, a double bed was crammed in between a solid pine dresser and a chest of drawers. A door at the opposite end of the space opened to reveal a smaller room. She was not surprised to see an old fashioned bathroom, though thankfully the toilet appeared to be a more modern addition and, on trying the hot water tap in the claw foot bath, the instant hot water suggested a new boiler hidden somewhere behind one of the numerous pine cupboards downstairs.

She went outside and dragged her suitcases in, she admitted defeat immediately, no way would she get them upstairs with their contents intact. She wondered how they had got the furniture up, maybe it had been built up there, she was sure she had read something like that somewhere, it might be something to look into though as she could see it being a sticking point for potential buyers. Over the course of the next few hours she would traipse up and down carrying her belongings to the bedroom, but first, she decided to begin a more in depth exploration of the ground floor.

Keys in hand she headed into the kitchen and found the key to unlock the back door. Once the door was opened and had let a little more light into the room she had discovered that the cottage had far more modern conveniences than she had anticipated. Carefully hidden behind pine cupboard doors were a fridge, freezer, washing machine, and microwave, most impressive were the radiators, carefully hidden behind wooden panels which she assumed were designed to let the heat out while being safe, another thing on her list of things to check out before she risked turning them on. Everything in the kitchen was hidden to create the illusions of belonging to a bygone age while requiring the occupier to do none of the hard work.

She had had the foresight to pick up the basic essentials such as bread and milk, and of course coffee, by slipping the taxi driver an extra few pounds to take a detour via the nearest shop. She had been relieved to realise it was little more than a fifteen minute walk from the cottage to the main street of the village, though probably another fifteen from there to the station.

The shopkeeper had been naturally curious at a new face across the counter but there was something that passed across his face when she mentioned why she was here. She could not exactly put a name to the emotion and anyone less inclined to paying attention to the details would have missed it, but she had definitely seen the shadow that had briefly passed across his face before it was replaced with a smile and what appeared to be a heartfelt welcome to the community.

It was early when she arose the next morning, a thin shaft of intense sunlight had crept between the edges of the curtains and bathed her face in golden light which had awoken her. She was amazed at how well she had slept, she had expected the thought of sleeping in a dead woman's bed to keep her awake. Whether it was the fresh country air or fatigue brought on by the days travelling, she had fallen into a deep slumber almost as soon as her head had hit the pillow. For the first time since discovering the infidelity she had slept soundly and without tortuous dreams plaguing her.

Feeling refreshed she decided to delay her planned exploration of the village and shopping trip, and take advantage of the early morning sun. Throwing on leggings and an oversized t-shirt, she slipped her feet into her pumps then carefully descended the stairs. The living room was dark but as she pulled back the curtains it seemed like the windows let in more light today. She wondered if it was just the positioning or strength of the sun, but it really did seem like the ivy was covering less of the glass.

She shook her head, of course that was not possible she thought to herself as she filled the old fashioned kettle and placed it on the gas hob. While she waited for it to boil she went back to the living room to retrieve her easel and painting supplies from where she had dumped them on her arrival.

Going out of the back door she stood and looked at her surroundings, the garden would once have been beautiful, but now slightly overgrown it had taken on a life of its own and was breath-taking. Colours bled into each other as previously defined borders had broken down and nature had weaved her own magic into man's design. She could see a well further down the path, and statues peeked out from behind waves of blooms. She decided this would be her project for her time here, she would paint the cottage and the garden now in the glorious state of wilderness before some new owner came along and hacked it all back, taming it into the regulation beds, that would make it like a standard cottage garden, or worse still, dug it all up to add a patio and tennis court.

For one brief moment she panicked questioning if she had the talent to capture the magic of the place, but just as quickly she dismissed the thought as a sense of belonging and confidence filled her. She had never believed in fate, yet at that moment she could think of nowhere else she could ever be, and nothing else she would ever want to paint as much as she did the sight before her. The whistle of the kettle pulled her back to reality and she headed back to the kitchen.

Coffee in hand she returned to the garden five minutes later and began picking out the views she would use to create a series of paintings. Out of the corner of her eye she saw two small figures, children she guessed, but they were gone before she could look round properly. She smiled assuming they were local kids curious to see who was living here, they would reappear at some point she was sure of it.

She decided to begin by painting a view of the full garden, literally painting just outside the back door so that it would recreate the view as she had first seen it. In the afternoon when the light moved she would begin a second canvas with the reverse view from the bottom of the garden. She was satisfied that these two paintings would help her get a feel for the place and provide the basis for the series of pictures just in case there was a quick sale on the cottage, though already she was hoping that would not be the case, she could happily spend her whole summer here. She took up her paintbrushes and began.

She had been painting for several hours before she got the feeling she was no longer alone. She had been so engrossed she had not noticed the passage of time but the sensation of the hairs on the back of her neck rising had broken her reverie. Looking round she saw two children at the bottom of the garden, she presumed they were the same ones she had spotted earlier. She had no idea how long they had stood there, she assumed not long or she would have noticed them, and though at the time, she thought they must have been out of her range of vision for the painting, later, when she looked again she could not understand how she had missed them.

Her eyes met theirs briefly and she smile to let them know they were welcome, her stomach rumbled and she looked down at her watch, shocked to see it was well past lunch time. When she looked up they were gone again. It hardly seemed possible they could have disappeared so quickly from her eyesight, but not knowing the area, she did not know what hidden lanes were situated beyond the fence. Glancing once more at the canvas she had been working on she was satisfied with her efforts and turned her mind to food.

Lunch consisted of a tin of soup and a couple of slices of bread, and reminded her she needed to make the trip to the shops before she started painting again for the afternoon, if she lost track of time again dinner would be beans on toast and considering how hungry she still felt after eating, that was not something she wanted to deal with, country air was certainly agreeing with her she decided.

After moving her pots to the sink, she picked up her phone and sat on the bench, it was perfectly placed by the back door for sitting out with a morning coffee or a glass of wine in the evening she decided. She had texted her sister to reassure her of her safe arrival, she had been happy to discover she had a good if not perfect signal strength. She had thrown her phone back into her rucksack and not bothered looking at it since, now she saw the red missed call symbol flashing at her.

Bringing up the call log she saw three missed calls, all from her ex. She wondered why he was ringing, had he suddenly realised he had made a mistake? Was it that seeing the flat without her influence, he had been struck by the fact she was really gone and he wanted her back?

For a moment her heart pounded as she allowed the fantasy to fill her, but the image was still there when she thought of him, and she came back to earth with a crash. She reflected it was more likely he was checking she had moved all her things out, so he could either get it on the market or, more likely, move the life model in. His parents had bought him that flat before the area was fashionable, and though it was now worth twenty times what they had paid for it, he would never be able to afford to buy again in the same area.

She stared at the screen, internally debating returning the call or not, in the end she decided to get it over with, hopefully it would be the last time she would have to deal with him. The call was brief and to the point, a simple transaction where he acknowledged her input into the building and offered to compensate her for the losses she would incur by leaving the property. She almost laughed at him as he tried to sound business like but at that moment she knew two things, one that he had talked to his parents and secondly that he was moving the new woman in.

He was trying for damage limitation as far as their mutual friends were concerned, but also he knew she had more contacts in the art world than he did, and as always he was putting himself first. She was tempted to turn down his offer, to act insulted, but the money would cover half the cost of the six months she had paid on the storage unit, she told him to send the cheque to her sister's. She was about to hang up when curiosity got the better of him and he began asking questions about where she was and who she was with, he knew she had to be with someone, so who was it?

She cut him off mid-sentence, and turned the phone off for good measure. There was a land line here in the cottage, her sister could use that to keep in touch until she arranged to have her number changed.

She grabbed her keys and her rucksack, and was well down the lane that led to the shops she had stopped off at last night, when she realised she had not locked the back door. She hoped it was true you could leave your doors unlocked in these small villages, or at least her painting equipment in the back garden would make people think she had just popped inside, either way she would soon find out.

As well as the newsagents shop she had visited yesterday, there were the array of shops you read about existing in villages before a supermarket moved in and put them all out of business. A butchers, bakers, hairdressers, and a hardware shop. Shopping this way would prove to be an experience for her, though not an unpleasant one. She was used to city living, a quick run round the supermarket, anything you could possibly need within grasp to just throw in a trolley and a taxi home. Now her choices were limited but there was something about the personal touch that made the experience so much more meaningful.

The shopkeepers were all as welcoming as the man in the newsagents had been the night before but she still sensed a strange apprehension from them, though they only asked the usual questions one would expect. Only one question had really stood out and that was from the young girl assisting in the bakers, she had leaned over the counter as if not wanting to be overheard and asked if Rachel had seen or felt anything in the cottage. She had been happy to laugh it off and say no, but she felt bad for the girl as the older woman who owned the business had scolded her. She had insisted it was okay she was not offended, and that it if the little old lady who had died there made herself known, she would be sure to tell them.

After the embarrassment of watching the girl chastised and in the hope of changing the subject she had mentioned she was a painter and was hoping to do a series of paintings of the cottage. She ventured to suggest that if things went as well as they had this morning she might have time to do some of the village as well while she was there.

The older woman had smiled, then explained, years ago when her grandparents were children, there had been a painter who lived in the village; she had one of his paintings of the cottage on the wall in her living room. He had not been famous, in fact, she laughed, he reminded her of Van Gogh, slightly mad and trading his paintings to pay his way. Her grandparents said he was mad in a nice way though, told fascinating stories, people had liked the paintings so they had happily traded with him for them, it was only after his death she had seen a similar picture to the one that hung on her walls on the box of chocolates. Rachel smiled, delighted and told of her own recognition of the cottage from her own childhood.

The woman explained that her son had done some research into the painting and found that the one they owned was worth a modest amount, enough to make it worth insuring but not enough to retire on, that was how her son described it. She would never consider selling it but she sighed as she admitted that she knew, it would not stay in the family once it passed to the next generation. She said what had been more interesting was learning more about the artist himself, he was a member of a well off family, there had been no need for him to live the way he had, but once he had chosen that path his family turned their backs on him.

At that point the younger girl, who she had learned was called Sally, interrupted talking about how it was fate that she was living there, she protested, trying to explain that she was only the house sitter and would not be staying, she got the impression neither woman believed her.

Supplies firmly stashed in her bag she headed back, musing to herself that it really was as if she had stepped back in time. Both the butcher, and the baker, had offered a delivery service and she had swallowed down her laughter when she realised the butcher's boy actually delivered orders on a push bike with a chiller box attached to the handle bars. She decided she would feel too guilty adding to his load to order much that way, but did allow herself to be persuaded to take a weekly delivery of bacon, sausage, and free range eggs, freshly laid by the hens the butcher proudly boasted he kept out back.

Arriving back at the cottage she found everything more or less as she had left it, though she could not help but feel it seemed tidier than before, she was sure she had left the coffee cup in the sink, not rinsed it and left it to drain. She was sure nothing had been taken and, that if intruders had been in and felt the urge to tidy up, then she could handle that.

The afternoon painting session passed as quickly as the mornings had, and as the light began to fade she cleaned her brushes and looked at the two paintings she had worked on that day. Both were further advanced than she had expected them to be after just one session on each, it was as if her hands were in tune with their surroundings or painting a view they had painted a hundred times before. She felt like every brushstroke reflected its organic counterpart with the briefest of touches to the canvas and the garden had sprung to life in her painting.

A noise, like a foot shuffling in the gravel, made her look round and she saw the two children once again. It was the first time she had the chance to observe them properly, the boy looked around seven or eight and a couple of years older than the girl, the similarities in features suggested brother and sister. She would have described them as small for their ages, but what struck her most was their expressions, both of them looked so grave and serious.

She was a little taken aback but, guessing they might be scared at having been caught in their trespass, she smiled and motioned them forward to take a closer look as she presumed it was her painting which had captured their interest and they were curious. The boy gave a wane smile back while his sister moved behind him as if shy. In an attempt to ease the girl's discomfort, Rachel turned back to the painting and began talking about it, she talked about the light and the colours, keeping it simple and trying to think of things a child might find interesting. When she received no answer she looked over her shoulder to where they had been stood, but they were no longer there.

Puzzled she looked round, baffled by how they had moved without her hearing them, she came to the conclusion these children were used to having to be silent, maybe home life was what caused those expressions. She debated enquiring next time she went to the shops, but decided, until she knew more it would be best not to ask questions, she would hate to get the children into trouble.

She was still contemplating what had happened when the house phone rang, she left everything where it was and rushed to answer it, hoping it would not be someone wanting to view the property already.

Her sister's voice burst forth from the handset, a rapid fire monologue leaving no spaces for Rachel to interject, she gathered from the high octane discourse that her ex had visited her sister in person, using the excuse of dropping the cheque off as a cover for a fact finding trip. She could tell from the amused tone, her sister had played up on the whole situation, as her sister related the part of the conversation where she told him Rachel had gone to a nunnery and was considering taking the veil was too much and Rachel burst out laughing.

It exploded from deep within her, and she struggled to breathe as all the tension built up over the previous month left her body. Her sister was worried, begging Rachel to calm down, the more her sister panicked and started talking about hysteria the more Rachel laughed.

Eventually exhausted she collapsed onto the sofa and began the task of talking her sister out of coming to visit her. She reassured her she had not felt this good in a long time, and that a weight had been lifted and it had been the release she had needed. They talked for a little longer, she told her what she had learnt about the history of the chocolate box paintings and asked her sister to do a little research for her. The fact she had to ask reminded her of her mobile problem and her sister promised to get a new phone sorted for her that would allow her internet access, that was of course if she could find a network with sufficient coverage out there.

When they hung up both sisters felt that the cottage was proving to be a godsend for Rachel.

When she finally returned outside to gather her things together, she noticed the sunset, the colours were so vivid that the sky looked like an artist's creation, especially when compared to the city skies she was used to. She knew then she needed to capture this, and the sunrise, before she left, and that if she failed to do so she would regret it, possibly for the rest of her life. Tomorrow she would do her best to get images of both on her camera, but she knew that it would not do this spectacular scene justice. Turning her attention back to her equipment, she put the last of her paints and other bits into the toolbox she used to carry them about in, she reached down behind the box to grab the jam jar containing the turps she had been using to clean her brushes. It was gone.

She looked round expecting to find it within a few feet having tipped over and rolled a little way, she checked under the bushes in case it had rolled there, but nothing. Just as she was about to give up her search, as the final rays of the dying sun slipped beneath the horizon, a glint in the corner of her eye drew her attention.

Sitting on the edge of the well was the jar, the muddy coloured turps had been removed and the jar rinsed out, it was now filled with crystal clear water and an array of wild flowers. A few looked like they may have come from the garden but some she had not spotted as she had painted and she thought must have been picked elsewhere. *It must have been the children*, she smiled, any negative thoughts about their abrupt departure earlier disappeared, and they were forgiven completely. She thanked them out loud as she picked the jar up and headed to the door, she hoped they were hidden close enough to hear her.

After a supper of bacon and eggs she decided to head up to bed and read for a while. Normally she would have fired up the laptop and done the research she was itching to do, but now, out of contact with the cyber world she had selected a pile of books from the shelf in the living room. The range of books had surprised her, and she realised she had assumed it was an old woman who had lived and died here, but as she tried to recall the conversations she had with her sisters friend, she could think of nothing relating to the age of the dead relative. Carrying the books upstairs it also struck her that nearly all of the personal effects had been removed before her arrival, maybe the estate agent could fill her in when she finally met him.

She read for an hour but once more it seemed the country air was hurrying her to an early night, she turned the lamp off then moved down under the blankets but sleep did not come straight away, something was playing on her mind. It was the children.

It was more than their strange expressions and the way they came and went so silently, their complexions were pale, it was almost as if the sun had never touched them. She had seen them out in the sun though, so maybe it was a form of illness, maybe something that led to them being shunned by other children, though on reflection, the brief acquaintance hardly gave her an insight into their normal everyday life. Their clothes were old fashioned, not in a last season way but more like last century but not shabby or poor quality.

She considered, they could be traveller children; that might explain some of their reticence to step forward at her invitation, maybe they were more used to being chased away. If that were the case should she encourage them? Would it lead to their families following them and pressing themselves upon her? Possibly the children themselves were aware of that possibility and that was why they were keeping their distance? She dropped off to sleep with many ideas racing through her mind, none of them quite believable to her and several that she was aware made her acknowledge herself in a bad light. The night was a restless one.

The weeks passed quickly and she found she had settled into a routine, mornings seemed to begin with the sun waking her naturally, though she had managed to get up once or twice in time to catch the sunrise on her camera and to mix a few colour swatches to remind her of the colours should she fail to finish the paintings she wanted to do. Next on her daily schedule was coffee and breakfast, followed by a painting session, she had now completed three full paintings of the garden and had started a fourth concentrating on the well area.

The afternoon painting sessions had also seen three large canvases come to life with scenes of the cottage from different angles. She had now started wandering further afield taking her camera, sketch pads and smaller paint box, out and about, down the country lanes and into the village. Although she had originally envisioned a series of paintings of the cottage, she found herself getting excited about the prospect of capturing, what she considered to be, a dying way of life.

The children became a regular presence, although they still kept their distance and had not yet uttered a word to her, she began to consider the possibility that they could not speak, and so she kept up a friendly monologue in their presence which they seemed to enjoy, or at least they seemed interested in what she had to say. She would leave treats for them, but they would never take them while she was in sight, but whenever she left for her afternoon outings or went into the cottage, they would disappear and frequently a nosegay would appear later the same day. She began to wonder if it was the children who were also responsible for the fact that she had returned to the cottage on more than one occasion to find someone had put the pots from lunch away in the cupboard.

She had only taken one trip back to the station, she had caught the train to the nearest town to replenish her art supplies and pick up new canvases. They were the only things she really needed that she had been unable to get at the local shops, although the proprietor of the hardware shop had offered to order them in for her. He had excitedly written down the types of supplies she might need so he could send off for the various catalogues in order to be able to acquire them for her, just in case she decided to stay, he had added, and once more she found herself asserting that her stay was limited.

Despite her protests that she was only here temporarily she found herself daydreaming about staying, however the bubble was burst by a call from the estate agents arranging to bring people round for a viewing. She tidied up the house before they arrived and filled jugs with freshly cut flowers from the garden to brighten the place up, it was the first day she had been here, where the skies were slightly overcast and the windows seemed to let in less light. With fresh coffee brewing to add a homely feel she opened the door to them and retreated to the garden to work on one of the paintings that was almost finished.

She stood at her easel but for the first time since her arrival she felt unable to concentrate, she kept half an eye out for the children but whether they had seen or sensed something was different today, they did not appear. She mixed colours on her palette absentmindedly as she listened to the agent giving his spiel as he showed the potential buyers round. Her heart sank at the prices she was hearing discussed, then it plunged ever further as the young couple he was showing round discussed the potential they saw, and the changes they would inflict upon the cottage, if they decided to buy it.

Rachel realised that even if this couple did not buy it, her days here were numbered, she could not afford to buy the place herself and even if it failed to sell and they dropped the price it would remain out of her reach. Someone would rush in eventually and snap it up, she could not expect her sister's friend to keep paying her to stay here. The amount they had agreed on was more of a token gesture and, though the cheque from her ex had covered most of the storage fees in the end, she had now started in on the scant savings she had. Every day she stayed here, the dream of living here for real, slid further away.

The rest of the day she found herself restless, unable to settle to anything. By evening she was feeling despondent. She grabbed a sketch book, glass, and bottle of wine, then headed to the bottom of the garden. There was a bench sat back into a nook at the end of the path, it had a view back up to the cottage, but provided a slightly different perspective to the ones she had produced so far. She curled up on the bench pulling her legs underneath her, and poured a glass of wine, she took a long, slow drink, allowing the flavour to stimulate her senses, then put the glass down, picked up the sketch pad and began to outline her view

. In a short while the pile of ripped out, discarded pages was building into quite a pile next to the rapidly emptying bottle, and she wondered if her productive stay in the cottage had come to an end.

She looked up and noticed the children sat on the edge of the well looking at her. Head tilted to one side, she found herself pouring her heart out to the two children as her pencil danced across the paper. On sheet after sheet the two children reappeared, almost like practised artist models, they moved poses after a period of complete stillness, as they continued to watch her.

Only once she closed the sketch pad and held it close to her chest did they finally move and approach her for the first time. Silently they moved towards her, and though she could clearly see them walking, they made very little noise on the gravel path as they approached, they gestured towards the sketch book, so she laid it in her lap and opened the pages.

Looking at them now she could see she had captured them perfectly, better than she thought herself capable, the melancholy air of their expression, their old-fashioned, quirky clothing. She found herself staring deep into the boy's eyes and she was filled with sadness.

She wanted to speak, to say something that would ease the pain she saw there, but words seemed woefully inadequate, but it was from the girl she heard the first word, so faint she thought she had imagined it, a single word 'stay', not a command but a plea. She looked across into the girl's eyes and almost immediately she wanted to pull her gaze away.

It was like staring into the abyss, into the darkest depths of the ocean, as if time itself had stopped and nothing else existed except this moment. This exact fraction of existence incorporated everything; all that stretched out into the future, every moment from the past, all possibilities were trapped here and existed in the sea green calm of the girl's eyes. She felt herself sway, the physical movement of her body pulling her back to her senses.

The girl was studying her and slowly a smile spread across the pale lips. Rachel looked down at where the pencil rested against the paper, thinking to take a moment to regain her composure, but as she looked down she saw the drawing and began to tremble. There was no way she could have made such a detailed sketch, even if she had been concentrating but she had no recollection of even making a mark. Her hand was shaking as she looked up again but once more the children were gone.

The next two weeks flew by but she hardly saw the children at all and then they kept their distance. Then the weather changed and several days running she was limited to the confines of the cottage as it rained constantly.

She had discovered that the living room lights were on dimmer switches on her arrival, but now she found that if she pushed them in as she turned they had a wider range, and was delighted to discover that she could actually brighten up the room considerably. Rather than test the central heating she decided to light the fire, and as the flames flickered they gave off a warmth that permeated her soul. She saw nothing of the children but that did not surprise her, after all, she would have been shocked by any parent letting their children out in weather like this.

She stood before the easel putting the finishing touches to a painting of the children. Rachel had arranged all the canvases she had created during her stay around the living room, it had seemed small in there before but now it was positively cramped, but it did not bother her in the slightest. She was amazed by her own work, it was the best she had ever produced.

Her sister had called the night before, the couple who had been to look round had put in an offer for the cottage and it had been accepted. She had one last week to finish off her paintings and vacate. The idea of leaving had reduced her to tears before she had reminded herself that it was like any other holiday, she had known from the start it was temporary and she would soon settle down to her normal existence once back in the city.

She stood back as she added the final brush stroke to the canvas. She had made this painting larger than the others, it was a full view of the garden with the children stood by the well, it had seemed appropriate this should be the centre piece of an exhibit.

The next few days she immersed herself in organisation, she emailed her agent photos of some of the other canvases, but this larger one she would let her see in person. She was thankful to her sister for the USB dongle that gave her internet connection though she had hardly used it and it had been temperamental at best but it now helped her get everything sorted.

She had instructed her agent to find her gallery space, she would exhibit the pictures of the cottage and its gardens, there were several of the village she would also include but the real stars would be the children. She wished they would call in so she could tell them the news but the weather had not relented, still there were three days left before she would leave and she hoped the weather would break so they could appear again before then.

The morning of her final day the sun broke back through the clouds. She took her coffee and sat outside in the garden one last time, savouring every moment. Her suitcases were packed and the taxi to the station was booked, a courier had called yesterday to take the paintings back to London.

She had broken up the last of the bread and watched as the birds nipped to the ground and grabbed a morsel before flitting up to the branches of the fruit trees situated along one side of the garden.

Then she saw them, standing where she had first seen them. As they approached, the early morning sun played tricks with her vision, it looked almost as if they were surrounded by light, no that was not it, almost, for a moment, they looked like they were part of the light.

She shook her head, clearing her vision, and they now stood before her smiling, their normally pale faces seemed to have more colour today. She found herself avoiding looking straight into their eyes, the memory of drowning in their gaze on their previous encounter resurfacing. Instead she looked at the tiny hand which now extended towards her, it was holding out a posy of wild flowers. As she took them she flinched involuntarily as her fingertips came into contact with those of the girl.

The small hand was cold, freezing, for the few seconds when they had made contact it had been like plunging her fingers into icy water. She raised her eyes to the smiling face, the girl looked so serene, as if all the worries Rachel had believed had plagued them during their acquaintance had been all in her own imagination.

Whatever hardships these two children had faced in their lives, today they were contented, perhaps she wondered if the freedom of the fresh air, after a week or so of being cooped up by the bad weather, had brought the colour to their cheeks. Or maybe their home life had just improve, whatever the cause, she felt her heart lift a little knowing they seemed happier, and in better health.

She had worried about whether her departure would upset them and wondered if there was a way to keep in touch with them so she could keep an eye on their progress, and maybe they could come to the opening night of the exhibition when she arranged things. She did not want to pry into the family situation, which given their silence during their visits, she did not expect them to talk about anyway.

She had finally asked several of the shop keepers about the children, but no one seemed to know who she was talking about, although she suspected they were not being entirely truthful from the looks that crossed their faces at her questions. This had led her to conclude that her first thoughts about them coming from a traveller family or some other less than desirable background may be true. She had decided in the end to leave a letter in the cottage for the new owners, it gave her sisters address and a description of the children and asked if they didn't mind, would they drop her a line occasionally letting her know how the children looked.

The girl tilted her head to one side, as if considering her words, then spoke in a surprisingly clear, loud voice.

"Don't be sad, you will be back soon, and we will be here when you return."

Rachel opened her mouth to protest, to explain that she would not be back, but instead she closed her mouth, smiled and nodded. What harm was there in letting them believe she would be back, the new people would move in, and no doubt the children would befriend them as they had her. She would be forgotten, other than as an occasional comment, when they looked back at their childhood in later life.

She stood up and said her goodbyes, she was surprised by the emotion these two urchins had inspired in her, their contact had been brief and their exchanges mainly one sided but she could not explain it, the feelings were there. She longed to reach out and hug the children but she held back, they had never demonstrated a desire for any type of physical contact and even as she said her farewells they seemed to be backing away down the path.

The gallery was packed, as soon as her agent had seen the full series of paintings she had swung into action, and less than a month after her return to the city, Rachel found herself at the opening night of her first major exhibition.

She stood in the corner of the room, concealed by a curtain, a glass of champagne clutched in her hand. It was the same glass she had been holding an hour ago and was now flat and far too warm to drink but it stopped anyone forcing another one on her.

The evening was a success, already over half the paintings had sold stickers discretely placed upon them. The only thing that had threatened to spoil the evening had been the appearance of her ex.

He had managed to manipulate a mutual friend into bringing him along as their plus one, she had been out of the country at the time of the break up and not known the full details. He had pretended he had realised his mistake, and that he wanted a chance to beg Rachel's forgiveness. The friend had been mortified to learn the truth about the situation and had stood by watching as his pathetic pleas for another chance, which at one point Rachel had longed so much to hear, were met by stony silence.

She had heard from friends upon her return that he had broken up with his model, and guessed his regrets were more likely attributed to his empty bank account, and reports of her expected success, than any real desire to win her back. He had tried to engage several agents, including her own, in conversation and had left after being snubbed on each occasion, she had almost felt sorry for him, he would never realise that charm could not take the place of talent.

She saw her agent motioning to get her attention and drawing herself up strode back out into the throng, her agent stood with a middle-aged woman who appeared to have photographs clutched in her shaking hands. Her agent had a puzzled expression on her face as she suggested that Rachel should take the woman through to the office in the back where they could talk properly. She shook her head at Rachel's quizzical look, explaining that this was something she needed to hear for herself.

Rachel gestured for the woman to follow before leading the way, threading through the other guests until they reached the office door. She swung it open then stood back and allowed the other woman to enter first.

The woman sat on the guest side of the desk leaving Rachel no option but to slip round behind the desk and into the large, leather chair her agent normally occupied. It gave her the opportunity to look at the woman properly for the first time, although she had initially thought the woman was middle-aged it now became clear she was older, late fifties, perhaps early sixties. She obviously took pride in her appearance, and her skilfully applied make up helped with the illusion of looking younger, as did the style of the skirt and blouse she wore.

At first glance she would not have stood out from the other guests, only on closer inspection would anyone have worked out she was not one of the affluent buyers, her bag and shoes had the look but not the labels of a designer lifestyle. The other thing that gave her away was the fact she only glanced at the paintings of the cottage, it was the paintings of the children that held her attention. Clutched in her trembling hands were a number of photographs, they looked old, tattered and worn, as if they had been lovingly handled by generations of hands, not just the manicured fingers that held them now.

"You wanted to talk to me? I am guessing you are not from the press?"

"No! I mean no, I'm not press, but yes, I do want to talk to you. I needed to come and see you and talk, but I am afraid that once I start you will think me mad and throw me out. So instead, I want you to look at these, then I will tell you a story, please…"

The last word trailed off as she gestured to the photographs, as she spoke she laid down four photographs onto the table in front of Rachel.

As she had suspected they were old, the first showed a family group, sat in front of the cottage. There were around thirty figures, every person was carefully placed around an imposing elderly gent who drew the attention of the eye by his central positioning. It was hard to make out the features of those at the back, years of handling had taken its toll on the images, but there was no mistaking that this family group were sat in front of the self-same cottage she had painted so much recently.

The next picture was a smaller family group, once again the elderly gent sat in the centre, but this time surrounded by children aging, she guessed, from three to twelve. She was about to move onto the next photograph when one pair of eyes caught her attention. She picked it up and looked more closely, there in amongst the others, were the children from the cottage. They looked younger than she had seen them, but those eyes were exactly the same, *no, they were children who resembled the children from the cottage, after all this was an old photograph, how could it be them?*

She looked up at the woman but received only a gesture to continue and look at the other pictures. The next showed a group of eight children, including the two from the cottage, she could no longer deny they were the same children, though she had no idea how this could be. The other children in the picture looked similar enough that it was obvious they were all related, they were all smiling. In this photograph the children looked exactly as she had seen them at the cottage, they were the right ages, and even wore clothes she recognised, though they looked newer in the picture than when she had seen them. Her mind was still trying to desperately claw for a logical explanation but she was failing to find one.

The final photograph was a studio portrait of the two children on their own, the girl perched on a chair, her brother beside her, his hand resting on her shoulder. She felt a cold shiver run down her spine as she thought of the painting hanging in the centre of the gallery. It showed the children positioned in that exact same way, but the chair had been replaced by the well wall.

The older woman seemed to notice her shudder and reached over and placed one hand over Rachel's which was now resting on the table, her other hand moved over the photograph where it had fallen, her fingers tracing over the familiar faces.

"It was the well painting I saw first, I don't need to tell you it was the picture used to promote the exhibition obviously." She gestured around them before continuing. "I saw a poster on a bus shelter as I was sitting under the dryer in a hairdressers, the woman came over to ask if I was alright, she said I looked like I had seen a ghost. I laughed at her when she said it, she had no idea how right she was, but how do you tell someone you have, unless of course, they have too."

Rachel tried to organise her thoughts, she had so many things she wanted to ask but, at the moment, felt incapable of putting a coherent sentence together, the other woman was smiling at her and nodding.

"I think I can imagine how you feel right now, but maybe it will be easier if I tell you what I know first, then we take it from there."

"Yes. Please, I need to know, I need… I don't know, right now, I don't know what to think, none of this makes sense, but it all makes sense. I…" Rachel found she could not find the words to express her emotions, and she was thankful, that this woman sitting across from her, seemed to understand.

"The man sat at the centre of the first two photographs was my great, great, grandfather, he built and lived in the cottage you stayed in." She now pointed to the youngest child in the first photograph. "That is my grandfather, he was the last child born in that generation, and this photograph was the last picture of all the grandchildren together with their grandfather. I am sorry I fear this may get confusing with all the generations."

"Please don't worry, I will stop you and ask if I get confused, can I ask though is the painter part of this story?"

"He was part of the family but not really part of the story, only in the fallout afterwards, but let's not rush ahead, where was I? Ah yes, the last full family gathering, times were hard but my great grandfather was determined to give his children the best start in life, even if that meant moving away from the rest of the family."

She had pointed to a man stood at the edge of the photograph, her finger delicately picking him out before pushing the first photo away and pulling the second to the fore.

"Just after the first photo was taken he packed up his family and moved to London, he took a job working on a market, as you can imagine long hours and no free time as such. This photograph was sent to him by his father to make him feel guilty that he had not been there the next year for the family gathering. His father had not been able to accept that he could not simply pack up and come home when he chose.

The final photograph was taken when my grandfather's cousins had come up to the city on a visit. He always told me how much he loved all his cousins but especially these two, Charles was always laughing and playing pranks, Lottie, or Charlotte, as she was christened, was much quieter, she was very much her brothers shadow. My grandfather cried the first time he showed me this photo, he had no idea it would be the last ever picture of them... well not quite, but the last of them living."

She paused, it was evident she was preparing herself for the final part of her story, the pain her voice had imparted in that last sentence suggested that it was as if these were her memories as much as her grandfather's.

"The last time he saw them there were tears all round, and promises that they would all meet up again at the cottage for Christmas no matter how hard it was to make it happen, but it was not to be. It was about a fortnight after they said goodbye at the coach house, the children had been playing in the garden, no one is really sure what happened next. The children were found at the bottom of the well, Charles was laying on top of Lottie; they guessed she had fallen in and he had fallen in after her, I like to think he was trying to save her when he fell.

My grandfather said it devastated his grandfather, that he bricked up the well and shut himself away becoming a recluse. He blamed himself, nothing anyone said could persuade him it was simply a tragic accident. The artist, my grandfather's uncle became obsessed with painting the cottage, it was as if he believed he could bring them back, but maybe it was something more.

Now you understand the irony of the position you painted them in, it could have been them in their final living places. I can see the look on your face, the denial and refusal to believe what I am telling you, even though you know it is true, but bear with me for just one more minute. Please."

The woman stopped speaking and opened her handbag, after a few seconds rooting about in it she pulled out another photograph, this one was more modern than the others though still showing signs of being well handled.

"My granddad visited the cottage several times as he grew up, he heard stories of people seeing his cousins but he never saw them himself. Years passed the cottage passed from the one member of the family to another, but no one stayed there for long..."

The woman noticed a puzzled expression on Rachel's face and raising a hand to silence the question she knew was imminent, continued.

"Oh, don't get me wrong it was never sold, how could it be sold if they were still there? The deeds expressly state that it must remain in the family, that spouses could remain in the property but they were never on the deeds, and once they left or passed away the property passed to the nearest blood descendant. Only if no more direct relative existed could the house be sold. And yes, I am aware of the reason you were there and I will come back to that after I finish, is that okay."

Rachel nodded, she had a hundred questions but needed to hear the rest, her mind raced as she tried to make sense of the story unfurling before her.

"The last relative to live there only lived in the house a few years before her passing, she had inherited from her father, he was one of my mother's cousins, but again he only lived there a few years. The cottage, from what I have heard in the family, does not always welcome people.

I have never set foot in it but my father did and he hated it. He refused point blank to live there when it was offered to my mother years ago. It would have broken my grandfather's heart, that refusal, he always loved the place and I could not understand how two men, so similar in every other way could feel so differently about one place. My mother was devastated but she abided by her husband's decision, convincing herself it was best for her family but as you will hear she never really forgave herself for not pushing harder over it.

But I am wandering again, and really I need to tell you everything. Over the years the instances of people saying they had seen the children diminished, or maybe they just saw two children in the distance and did not understand the significance to comment on it but either way my grandfather's health was beginning to fade and he decided he wanted one last visit. He insisted my mother and I join him. I was only young at the time, but I can remember how my father protested but my grandfather won, he said it would be the last time he went and he wanted to put his mind at ease, lay the ghosts to rest as he put it, except, that is not what happened."

She passed the photograph she was holding to Rachel, it showed an old man, who bore a startling resemblance to the old man in the older photographs, standing at the gate to the cottage with a young girl. She did not immediately notice the other figures but as she searched the picture she saw them, stood at the very edge of the camera frame. They stood just at the side of the cottage where the path led round to the back and appeared to be watching proceedings with an undisguised curiosity. Rachel's eyes remained fixed on the children while the woman began speaking again.

"We did not see them while we were there, it was only after the photographs were developed that we spotted them. My grandfather was so upset, he was convinced he should have seen them, my mother spent hours trying to persuade him that it was just meant to be that way, maybe they no longer had the strength to appear in plain sight only to imprint themselves through the camera. She had wanted to go with us that last time, and from everything she said to me I had thought she didn't really believe despite the photograph. She had taken it, and swore she saw nothing as she pressed the button, and I believed her. Or at least that's what I thought until she saw an advert for your exhibition.

The phone was ringing when I got home from the hairdressers, she had seen your advert about the same time I had. I had to ask her to slow down several times as it all came blurting out, her confession if you will. She admitted she had seen the children herself when she was little but she said when she saw them they always seemed so sad. She said in your painting they looked so happy and content, that is part of the reason I am here, as silly as it will sound to you, she needs to know if that is how they really are? Are they happy now? Are they content, at peace?"

"I don't know what to say," Rachel's voice cracked as she spoke, "I thought they were real children, strange children yes, but they never seemed anything other than rea…"

Her voice trailed off as she considered the thought that had passed through her mind, silent comings and goings.

"If anything the longer I was there the more real they became, at first they were silent, they kept their distance. I just thought they were just shy, the longer I was there the more they interacted with me but never anything personal. They would not tell me their names even, if I asked about family they clammed up, but they seemed to like being there and being around me."

Rachel's face flushed as she thought about the assumptions she had made about the children's home lives.

"Thank you!" She passed the studio photo to Rachel, "I would like you to keep that, and, as I am the last descendant of the family, and I have no one else to pass the photos onto, I would like to bequeath the others to you when the time comes. I am sure you can understand why I want to keep them with me for now.

Rachel nodded. "But you must have something in return, you can give it to your mother if you don't want it for yourself."

She stood and led the woman back into the gallery, quickly she located her agent and after a few words were exchanged she motioned for the woman to join her by a smaller canvas, one of the few yet to sell. It showed the garden painted from just outside the kitchen door, the well featured in the centre of the picture but it was the two small figures sat in the distance on the bench that she knew was the real attraction.

"I want you to take this, think of it as a trade for the story and the photograph."

"I can't accept this; it is far too valuable."

"Yes, you can! After all, if it wasn't for your family there would be no painting and certainly no exhibition, and even if I had painted the cottage it would not have been as successful if it had not been for two certain children." A rueful smile crossed her lips, "I just wish it had happened sooner, my agent informs me that other than this canvas I am giving you, only two others remain to be sold. Ironic isn't it,

I could actually buy the cottage outright now without even needing a mortgage with the profits from the sales. But it is sold, nothing I can do about that."

"No, it's not. I told you the house can't be sold, the solicitor dealing with things for your friend had not looked into the clauses carefully enough, she inherited through a blood relation but she is not. They did not have the power to leave it to her while blood relatives survived, the cottage belongs to my mother, then it will pass to me, then there is no one else."

Rachel felt the room close in on her as emotions threatened to overwhelm her senses, the woman reached forward and took her arm, holding her steady as she continued her disclosure.

"I have talked it over with mother, we have no intention of living there, and I feel sorry that your friend had her hopes raised and then we had to disappoint her. So we have the answer, you will buy the cottage from us but the money will go to your friend, we don't need it we have enough to finish out our days comfortably. You will pay eighty percent of the market value to her, the only thing we want you to agree to is finding a way to ensure the cottage remains as it is, that you continue to protect the children, and maybe you let me come and visit occasionally."

"Thank you! Thank you!" Rachel threw her arms around the woman the force almost taking them both off their feet, when she finally released her, tears of happiness streamed down the cheeks of both women.

Rachel stood watching as the removal van pulled away, there had not been much to unload as she had found the contents of the cottage included as a job lot when the paperwork for the sale had been finalised. She had laughed, knowing that in part, it was because no one else had figured out how the bed had got upstairs in the first place and they had all decided against trying to find a way to get it out.

The exhibition had been a complete success with all the painting sold and, after costs, her agents' commissions and the purchase of the house there was still enough in the bank to live on for a while. The confectionary company that had bought out the chocolate factory who had used the cottage on their chocolates had been in touch, they wanted her to update the image, a painting of the cottage but with a modern twist and of course there were those sunsets she had not managed to get round to painting

The crunch of gravel under foot pulled her attention back from her daydreams and she looked towards the side of the house where two small children had just raced round the corner, bright smiles on their faces and a flush of colour in their cheeks would fool those who did not know their story. She was not exactly sure how this was going to work but she was confident that together they would find a way, cold hands clasped hers and together the three of them went inside to begin a new chapter.

THE BROADCAST

Sir Henry Huntington-Smythe stared out of the window at the people scurrying below. He had been watching them for the past hour, and his annoyance had grown in proportion to their coming and going.

"Damn fool idea, and I get the blame for it. Trying to claim I blew the family wealth gambling, when we all know it was young Harrington that lost it all on the stock market years later, acceptable to lose thousands on stocks, and a scandal to lose a few guineas at cards."

"You didn't just lose a few guineas though did you? You lost half the estate, the horses and the carriages as well!"

The woman who answered him back sounded bemused as she berated him.

"It doesn't matter anyway who lost it, the fact is the money is gone, and unless something changes, the family will lose the house. I do not approve of this latest scheme of theirs, but what can we do?"

"Do! Do! I tell you what we can do, nothing, we do nothing! We do not co-operate with them in anyway, we do not speak to them, appear for them, or perform their parlour tricks, we do nothing! We have noble blood running through our veins,

and they are expecting us to act like performing monkeys for these, these…peasants!"

"And if we do as you say and do not interact, what do you think will happen?"

She rolled her eyes at him.

"I will tell you what will happen, they will take their money back, and the new guest house venture will fail, and this building will be sold and divided up to make smaller dwellings. I have heard the staff talking, they are all discussing what will happen, they will be out of jobs and we will have to share our home with dozens of people crammed in different rooms, strangers rather than family.

You might want to think about that before the others gather to find out what your plan of action for this evening is. I am sure the idea of your beloved study, stripped bare and turned into a kitchen, is something you would wish to avoid."

She flew out of the room through the wall next to the fireplace leaving Sir Henry to consider her words.

Below in the entrance hall, the living residents of the house were deep in conversation with the television director who was in charge of making sure this evenings filming went smoothly.

"So how many ghosts did you say there were here? "

The man held a clipboard and was scribbling notes frantically in between continuing this conversation, barking instructions through a headset, and half a dozen other jobs he seemed to be managing simultaneously.

"Six regular ones and several others that visit occasionally. The main ones, as we mentioned in our previous phone conversations, are Sir Henry and Lady Georgiana."

"And they were married?"

"No! Sir Henry lived here in the 1600's and died after falling from his horse while drunk, Lady Georgiana was late 1700's and we think died from consumption."

"No, she died from a broken heart dear."

The woman placed a hand on her husband's arm as she corrected him, smiling as a dark shadow of annoyance passed over his face. Lady Rosalind, last of the bloodline and great great granddaughter of Lady Georgiana, sighed gently.

The stories had been passed down the generations, she had married for love and it had turned out her husband had been a money grabbing bounder, he had disappeared with her jewels and the scullery maid. Lady Georgiana had only discovered she was carrying a child after his departure, and it was from their son that Rosalind was descended.

At times Rosalind wondered if she had made a similar match, although she knew there was no chance of Charles disappearing with the family jewels, they had all been replaced with paste and glass years before they came into her possession.

The television show had been her husband's idea, as was phase two of his grand plan, which he planned putting into action as soon as filming was finished. He intended, by the time the programme was aired, that they would be ready to host haunted themed weekend parties, with people paying large amounts of money to be scared witless.

The main problem as she saw it was the ghosts they had were not really scary at all, or at least she didn't think they were, they were just elderly relatives who happened to be dead, she had always sensed them.

Charles on the other hand never saw or felt any of them but he did know they were there, they made sure of it, they really did not like him at all, though, for her sake, they would never actually harm him they did plague him incessantly in small ways, especially Sir Henry, and Claudia.

Claudia was a new ghost and not as strong as the others, Rosalind suspected she would not remain long and would eventually move on wherever it was they went. She had only passed five years ago, it had been a terrible time, she and Charles had only been married a few months and they had barely returned from their honeymoon when tragedy struck. Claudia lived in the house, running the grounds and doing her best to keep the place afloat, while Rosalind brought in extra income by doing graphic design for an advertising agency in London.

The arrangement had suited them both, but Charles had not been tactful in his suggestions that Claudia should move out when he moved in. He wanted to take over the running of the estate and had wanted her to work from home, to maintain the appearance of them being gentry. He would have demanded she give up her job but it had only taken one look at the books to convince him that was not practical.

Claudia had been out riding alone when something had spooked the horse and she had been thrown. It seemed natural to Rosalind that her cousin should hang around, Charles thought it was in bad taste, now Claudia spent much of her time deliberately annoying him by moving his belongings. This morning he had spent an hour searching for his cuff links before the cook sent them up with an enquiry as to why they had been in the fridge.

She was drawn back from her own thoughts by the nudge of an elbow in her ribs.

"They were just asking about triggers for making your ancestors appear? Told them just about anything sets them off, told them over sensitivity runs in the family."

Charles laughed as if he had just made a hilarious joke, both the director, and his wife exchanged embarrassed looks.

"Maybe you could take a walk round with our technician, point out the best places to put sensors and fixed cameras while I get a few more anecdotal stories from your wife."

"Ah, help out the technical chaps, that sounds far more interesting that listening to her retell all those boring stories, again. Mind you once we start the haunted weekends here I will have to make sure she spices them up a bit, most of the family she has that hang around are distinctly boring, keep falling off horses."

Rosalind cringed at his last words, flung over his shoulder as he moved off to offer his assistance to an annoyed looking man, the look the technician fired towards the director left no doubt he considered he had received the short straw.

"Now it is just the two of us shall we go somewhere more comfortable and you can tell me the history of the house from a personal perspective and anything else you think might help us this evening. I know lots of people think this show is a joke, but the psychic we have with us is very good, he is a genuine guy. If you have any questions you want asking about, or any subjects you would prefer were not discussed, just let us know and I will put it to him, not promising any answers of course, that depends on your family, as it were, and how willing they are to help you."

"I have no doubt they would do anything to help me, just not so sure they will co-operate with Charles." She clasped her hand over her mouth, "Did I really say that out loud? Please ignore me. I just worry about things too much; I am sure they will provide you with enough footage for a great show."

She led the director into the morning room which also served as her office, and spent the next hour telling him the stories of her ancestors, and their history with the house and surrounding areas. When she finished the director seemed pleased, but she could not help but feel more apprehensive than she had when they had first arrived this morning.

After they had finished their conversation she retreated to the stables for the rest of the day, the house was a hive of activity as they set up, but it was more her husband she wished to avoid, only when she could no longer delay did she returned to the house, shower, and force herself to eat. She would have skipped eating as well had a cameraman not pulled her to one side and pointed out that she would not want her stomach to growl during the evening's filming.

There were eight of them now gathered in the tower room and the discussion had been becoming rather impassioned when Claudia stood to address them. As the youngest present at the meeting, in both mortal years and in time since her passing, she was treated like a child by the others, despite the fact her grasp on the modern world and the financial position of her cousin exceeded the knowledge possessed by the rest of them put together. Now however, they sat listening to her as she explained the whole concept of what would be happening in the house this evening. She explained the awkward position they were in, that while she had no desire to make life easy for Charles, her hatred towards him was overwhelmed by her love for her cousin.

"Things are so precarious at the minute we have no choice but to co-operate. Everything else has been tried and there is not enough money left in the pot for another venture, the bank has only accepted the latest extension on the mortgage because they can see that this idea of haunted weekends might work, otherwise they will foreclose on the house and it will be bought by developers. They were already putting in offers while I was alive. But I do have a plan, I think I know a way that we can make tonight work in our favour, rid ourselves of Charles and help Rosalind keep the house. We can make sure he does not profit from his schemes and though she might be upset in the short term, Rosalind will be happier than she is now and better off. Now are you interested?"

There was a general murmur of assent and then they listened intently as she explained her plans. Lady Georgiana stood back from the others, listening sadly at the discussions to destroy her descendant's relationship, she knew it was for the best. She already knew the secret Claudia was now sharing with the others, but it did not change the sadness she felt knowing the pain Rosalind would face before dawn.

The crew had everything set up, bundles of cables snaked along skirting boards and Rosalind dreaded to think what the electric bill would be, for despite the reassurances that they were using their own generators, it seemed every plug socket was in use.

She and Charles had spent an hour in make-up to record a five-minute slot for the introduction for the show, they had spent twenty minutes stood in front of the cameras and she had been surprised by how warm it was, she knew it would be cut down in the editing process, but part of her worried what they would create from the footage they had.

She hoped that the majority of what Charles had said would end up on the cutting room floor, but feared it would be kept in, she even mused about the idea of asking the director to intervene. If they wanted people to spend money staying here, then the less they saw of Charles beforehand the better. As usual he thought he was being witty and charming, but she had noticed the usual cringing from the people in hearing distance, and once more she found herself questioning how she had ever fallen for him.

She had been secretly pleased when the director had taken him to one side and suggested to him, purely from a business point of view, of course, that it should be she who would accompany the hosts on the walk round. He had tactfully pointed out that as she had inherited the title rather than gained it through marriage it would add more gravitas.

The fact the title was only on loan to him was a bone of contention. It was a sore point that had raised its head when the subject of children had been discussed, should they have a son, then on her death the title would pass to him and Charles would have to give it up, thankfully they had not brought a new life into this minefield that her marriage had become.

The director had reminded Charles that her knowledge of the family, and history, would come across better on the television, coming naturally to her as it were, and make people more likely to want to come to stay. It had been the pound signs represented by the last comment that had seen him agree to retreat to the mobile editing suite with the production staff, to make notes, as he put it, for use in the promotional material for the haunted weekends. In his mind this venture was already a success and he saw no end of money to throw at it.

She was introduced to the hosts of the show, a young woman in her twenties, Amelia, who appeared bored by the whole thing and spent most of her time on her mobile phone. The director had whispered into her ear not to take any notice and assured her that the woman would be attentive enough once the camera was rolling. He explained that Amelia was at the end of her contract and in line to be signed to host a daytime TV programme, however she had discovered only this morning another fan favourite from a reality TV show was also in the running and she had been harassing her agent ever since she had been informed of this gossip.

The other host was an older man, Shawn, there was a definite tension between the two hosts, and Rosalind gathered from the comments she overheard, it seemed the man was in a precarious position as discussions were taking place whether to replace him at the same time they found a replacement for his colleague, new faces and a fresh start were phrases she heard him repeat through gritted teeth to Amelia though she made a point of ignoring him.

The one person she immediately felt comfortable with was the medium, Damien. He was a huge bear of a man, well over six foot and well built, she wondered how he would cope with some of the narrower passageways. He was incredibly softly spoken and assured her he was agile enough to explore the house, anywhere they could get a cameraman through with his equipment, he would manage no problem. She found herself smiling genuinely for the first time in longer than she cared to consider.

He had kept his distance from everyone else, determined he did not want to hear anything which might influence him, she had been shocked by how much of what she had discussed earlier with the director, seemed to now, to be open knowledge between the hosts and the crew. She could not help but feel she had been a little gullible in her own viewing of the shows after Charles had revealed he had contacted them. She tried to think back to the hours she had spent watching in dismay at the thought of them traipsing round her home, but on reflection she thought, it was only ever the medium who claimed no prior knowledge, and she realised now, this was only due to his own integrity.

They began the filming with a quick tour of the house, filming short clips and items of interest in each area, several times she noted the hosts claimed to hear things that no one else picked up, and Damien remained quiet. Other than to acknowledge he felt there were spirits in the house who seemed unwilling to come forward, he was subdued, she wondered if his job was also at threat from the reshape, or whether he was aware of more than he was letting on.

She noticed furtive glances pass between the hosts and the director, and Rosalind could not help but wonder what they had planned, she just hoped whatever it was would not annoy her relatives too much, otherwise they may just find they got more than they bargained for.

Finally, all the preparations had been made, the introductions filmed and clips to camera recorded ready to be inserted later. The directors voice echoed throughout the house both into the room and through the headphones worn by crew, it was ten o'clock, time for the lights to go out!

They had set up the Ouija board in the main dining room, and the hosts wanted to begin with that but Damien resisted and decided he wanted to begin upstairs, reluctantly they acquiesced and the party alighted the main stair case. Rosalind felt unusually nervous, Charles was outside in the editing van once more, but something told her tonight was going to be a very long one.

As they entered Lady Georgiana's room Rosalind cringed as Amelia immediately began giving an over dramatic account of the history of the room, thankfully the medium silenced her, and began himself recounting a more realistic version of the life, and death, of the former occupant.

Lady Georgiana stood by her bed watching the performance unfold before her, she was aware the medium knew of her presence but at least he seemed respectful, she was also fully aware of Rosalind's discomfort. Her nature demanded she withdraw from the room but she reminded herself of the reasons they were going along with this. They were doing it for the good of the family and the house, and like it or not they had not come up with a viable alternative. She took what would have been a deep breath had she still been breathing, picked up her hairbrush from the dressing table and threw it at the male host.

The shock of the brush flying past his head caused Shawn to cry out, but his yelp was nothing compared to the scream let out by the sound engineer whose head the brush made contact with. Suddenly screams rang out in all directions, an emotional chain reaction and Rosalind found herself amused by the ensuing panic, after all they had come looking for ghostly goings on, and yet, at the first sign of activity they acted like scared school children.

The only person other than Rosalind who seemed unaffected by the drama was Damien who stood looking towards the dressing table. She wondered if he could see anything, although she regularly felt the presence of her ghostly family she very rarely saw anything, usually she only saw the objects they interacted with move, or the occasional shadow, it was always the fleeting, corner of the eye type of thing, sometimes she felt disappointed she could not see more of them.

As she followed the medium's gaze she was sure she saw the hand mirror lift a few centimetres before gently settling back onto the dressing table. Of course, she thought, Lady Georgiana would never be able to bring herself to throw something that might break, and instead the next wave of hysteria was caused by the chair next to the fire which began rocking violently of its own volition.

It was around twenty minutes, of screams and shrieks, later when the hosts and crew had regained most of their composure that they were ready to move on to the next room. The director was berating Damien via the headset for the lack of names, it seemed despite the evidence of a ghostly presence and his ability to give a description of her ladyship, it had not been enough. Damien had explained that the ghost had refused to speak to him and while Rosalind had confirmed the identity from the description she could hear Charles in the background ranting about her family and their lack of co-operation. She was glad the lights were down so no one could see the colour rise in her cheeks.

In the tower room the ghosts were in hysterics over the reactions that Georgiana had elicited, all except Sir Henry, he was still unhappy at the thought they were having to pander to the mortals, even if it was to save the family home.

Next up to put in an appearance was Sarah, by nature she was a shy creature, in life she had been a maid and under normal circumstances would have had very little contact with the more affluent spirits, but today Sir Henry had summoned them all to take part.

"But Ma'am, I don't think I can do it...'

Lady Georgiana stood before the girl and looked down at her, this was not natural to any of them and she felt guilty for asking them to do this but there was no alternative.

"Just do your best, you don't have to do lots just move a few things around, if it makes you feel better think of it as tidying up, just with people watching."

The maid managed a faint smile before disappearing through the wall and heading to the kitchen.

The heavy copper pans hung from the ceiling, and it took so much energy for Sarah to just move them a little, the hosts were calling out over and over again for her to repeat her actions but with each attempt the amount of movement she could produce lessened. Finally, her energy depleted, she collapsed in a sobbing heap next to the fireplace.

Damien moved to where she was curled and crouched down close to where he sensed her to be, he spoke so gently. His words were comforting and he asked her a few simple questions which her position, combined with the tone of his voice, made her forget she was not supposed to speak to him.

In between gulping sobs, she answered the questions he put to her, her name, position and the tragic tale of her death from a fever contracted during a visit home to visit her family in the nearby village, tears swelled in the eyes of the medium as he recounted her last hours alone in one of the outhouses, banished from the house for fear of infection.

Suddenly the pans clashed violently together, a deafening cacophony of sound, Sir Henry who had never once ventured into the kitchen during his lifetime did so now to make his anger known, Sarah fled through the walls ashamed at her indiscretion and fearful of the older ghosts' wrath.

Damien backed away and stood against the wall, Rosalind sensing that things were about to get very interesting followed his lead. The two hosts remained in the centre of the room, calling out and demanding that the spirits present make themselves known. Damien was trying to explain over the raised voices of the others what he was sensing and that several other spirits had joined them. He was appealing for the hosts to calm down and let him communicate with them but his request went unheeded.

Rosalind ran through her mental list of the resident ghosts trying to guess which ones would have joined them and what they could expect, but just as she had reassured herself that nothing really untoward could happen down here, Amelia opened her mouth. She launched into a tirade at the unseen presences and began accusing them of bullying the ghost of the maid. Rosalind swore under her breath, she had no idea how she knew but suddenly she saw with perfect clarity the figure at whom the comments had been directed, she grabbed Damien's arm and pulled him into an alcove.

The next few minutes were a blur as objects flew from several directions at once, Sir Henry was furious, he launched every item that was not secured in place at the hosts and the crew, numerous people cried out as they were hit by pans and utensils. The vigour with which items were launched seemed to increase in relation to the growing number of screams, and a camera man fell to the floor after being caught from behind by a frying pan. Rosalind seeing the cupboards start to open, stepped forward, and, just as the doors to the china cabinet began to swing ajar, raised both her hands in the air.

"Stop this right now! Enough is enough, firstly when you have quite finished, I am the one who is going to have to pick all this mess up and secondly, I am the one who will have to face the cook in the morning and explain why all these pans are dirty and dinted. But let me be quite clear about this, that is nothing to the tongue lashing you are going to get from Lady Georgiana if you smash so much as one plate out of that cabinet."

A final pan dropped to the floor at the back of the kitchen and the cabinet door closed gently. Both the living and the dead it seemed had been silenced by her outburst and she felt the colour rising in her cheeks once again, but she was distracted from her own self-consciousness by Damien, who was doing his best to stifle a laugh, and when everyone turned to him he explained what he had just witnessed. He described how four portly gentleman spirits had frozen in mid throw and all looked down at the ground like naughty school boys receiving a scolding from their nanny. Only one spirit did not feel suitably chastised by Rosalind's remarks, Sir Henry made a point of opening and slamming the door as he left the kitchen and retreated back to the tower room.

Midnight was approaching and they had several rooms they still wished to investigate and a séance to hold, it was decided they would split up. Damien would go with Rosalind and Amelia up to the nursery, while Shawn along with two of the camera men would remain on the main staircase and call out there, though given Sir Henry was the spirit most likely to be seen there in normal circumstances, Rosalind was doubtful they would find that vigil fruitful.

In the nursery they sat in a circle on the floor, this was one of the rooms Rosalind was sure they were most likely to get positive responses, she knew there was at least one ghostly child and she doubted Lady Georgiana would allow Sir Henry to intimidate the younger spirits to silence. Damien sat eyes closed describing a boy and a girl, he speculated they would have been around six and three but they had no interest in talking, though they were happy enough to roll back the ball Amelia sent bowling across the floorboards.

She had an idea who the girl was but not the boy, of course many children had been born and died her over the centuries and not all recorded but a six-year-old would certainly have been old enough to have his life and death marked. Through the headset she heard the director demanding a name for him and a story, for a moment she was sure she heard it suggested that they make up a name and a story, she was also sure it had been Charles voice she heard making the suggestion, but for now she focused on pushing him out of her mind.

Despite the lack of knowledge coming from the medium the crew appeared happy with the footage they were getting, the children had become bored with rolling the ball with Amelia and the boy now sat on the rocking horse pretending to be a knight in a jousting competition and the girl was rearranging the furniture in the doll's house.

The doll's house was a replica of the actual house though the number of rooms inside had been reduced, and the layout kept a lot simpler than it was in real life, Rosalind could not help but smile as she remembered her own childhood battles with the invisible playmate who had swapped the furniture into different rooms, as an adult she had come to understand they were changing it to suit the rooms as they had been during the child's life whereas she had always set it up from her own experiences.

The atmosphere had become more relaxed and the incident from the kitchen almost seemed forgotten until a scream tore through the house.

They ran from the room onto the landing and looked towards the main staircase where the scream had issued from. The lights came on and as they reached the top of the staircase they could see the prone figure of Shawn laying at the bottom.

The lights came on, and the director along with several other people, rushed into the building, Shawn was out cold, and concern over the severity of his injuries was the primary concern for most of the crew. Rosalind was trying to make sense of the sequence of events from the cameraman, he had been positioned at the top of the stairs, was now being interrogated by Amelia.

It seemed Shawn had been stood on the staircase, around three quarters of the way up, he had decided it was a good idea to call out and ask the spirits to push him, Rosalind shook her head, after the incidents in the kitchen she could not believe he had been so foolish. The next this anyone knew he was flying through the air, luckily rather than a straight push it appeared as if he had been picked up and moved down the stairs before being dropped from about a third of the way up.

Shawn was regaining consciousness, the thick rug that Rosalind had put that the bottom of the stairs had cushioned his landing, but his arm was twisted at an unnatural angle, and the pain was clear as he became aware of his surroundings.

At the same time, the young soldier, who had been killed during World War I, was being berated in the tower room by Sir Henry for taking the hosts request literally, his defence was that it was not his fault that they had not been more careful what they had asked for, and pointed out that if he had just pushed the man, it would be his neck that was broken, not just his arm.

An ambulance had been called and discussions were frantically taking place between cast, crew, and management. Several wanted to call it a night but the director was trying to calm everyone down and persuade them to film the final part, the séance.

The crew in the editing suite had confirmed the cameraman's story, and that it had all been caught on film. Amelia's face took on a green tinge, then gradually turned to scarlet with anger as she realised that her co-host had found a way to upstage her, the fact he had not done so willingly was lost on her. She knew now her only chance of getting the lion's share of airtime in this episode would be for a dramatic finale, she needed the chance to outshine Shawn and added her voice to that of the director in urging for a continuance of filming.

It was two in the morning by the time Shawn was on his way to hospital, sensing Amelia's plan for hijacking his spotlight he begged for extreme pain relief and to be able to continue, but in the end had been forced to accept that it was not an option.

The rest of the crew gathered in the dining room ready for the final vigil of the evening, the Ouija board had been placed in the centre of a small side table, a favourite of Rosalind's and she hoped that it would not be damaged in the séance. Initially, they had intended using the dining table, but it had become evident in the earlier walk round that people could not stand round it and place their fingers on the planchette. Nervously Rosalind now stretched her hand out and gently placed her finger on the tear shaped piece of wood, she felt a spark of electricity as her finger brushed against Damien's, static, easy to dismiss from her mind, after all she was a married woman.

Claudia stood by the wall waiting for her performance to begin, a wry smile crossing her face, she knew what she was about to do depended on the psychic actually relaying her message in full, but as she was sure it would make great viewing she was confident they would not only go with it but that they would also follow her directions to find the physical evidence. The connection between her cousin and the psychic had also not passed her by and though she knew he would keep it to himself she thought it could not help to let him know that he had her approval, well when the time was right of course.

Amelia now began recording a piece to camera, she was describing what they were going to do and then turned to Damien and asked him to let them know if anyone was present.

"There are several spirits in the room, they are all standing back, curious and something more, it is as if they are waiting for something, some specific event to happen. There is one stepping forward from the others, a young woman, late twenties, modern, I would say passed within the last few years."

"Claudia." Rosalind's voice was little more than a whisper.

Claudia moved to stand next to her cousin, knowing that what she was about to do would cause pain for her in the short term, but would protect both her income and her life, in years to come.

Amelia and Damien arranged the crew round the table ready to begin the séance, Rosalind glanced towards the area where the majority of the ghosts had gathered, a move that did not go unnoticed by Damien. He found it strange that she sensed the others but not this determined spirit who now stood by her side. Claudia winked at him, and then had to stifle a giggle as he blushed and missed his cue from Amelia to begin calling out.

They began now in earnest and Rosalind constantly glanced around the room, she could not see the spirits but she sensed them, but her brow furrowed as she realised her uneasiness was not at those present but at the ones who were absent. She could not sense the presences of Claudia, Lady Georgiana or Sir Henry.

The three spirits who she had expected to have the most to say appeared to have decided they would not participate, panic rose. In her chest her heart thudded as if it could break through her rib cage. Charles would be furious if this failed, she needed them to help her out now, especially after the incident earlier. She needed people to want to visit, experience ghostly goings on without feat of broken bones, she needed her ghostly family to do something now.

Charles had been watching the evening unfold via the monitors and up until this point had been pleased with the results but now he watched the look on his wife's face and concern began to develop. His feelings were not for his wife, he really could not care less how she felt, but he could see the pound signs receding as the psychic called out and nothing happened.

He rose to his feet intending to make an appearance of his own, hoping his presence would rile up the freeloaders who insisted on loitering without contributing anything to his bank account. He reached out for the door handle but it refused to move, placing both hands on the handle he tried brute force but nothing would shift it, crew members took turns but it would not give for any of them.

Frustrated he turned his attention back to the screen while crew members frantically tried to get help, on the outside of the mobile unit, crew members scratched their heads at the fact the door handle appeared to be frozen into place. It was so cold none of them could bear to touch it, let alone hold onto it for longer than a second or two. Sir Henry stood with a bemused but satisfied look, his hand firmly wrapped round the handle.

Claudia reached out and placed her hand on the planchette, it was time for the truth. Summoning all her energy she pushed the wooden pointer towards the letters that would begin the avalanche.

"M-U-R-D-E-…"

Damien called out the letters as the pointer paused upon them, Amelia let out a squeal of delight.

"Murder! Murder! That's the message, who is it? Can you see them? Can you tell who it is? Rosalind do you know who it could be?"

Amelia's excitement was obvious as she calculated the bonus air time these developments would bring over that featuring her injured colleague. The planchette resumed its journey across the board despite the fact no one was now in contact with it, they had all stepped back as that first word had been understood. It moved swiftly from letter to letter, only Damien keeping up with it enough to spell out the majority of the message.

"Car horn – deliberate – spooked horse – kept sounding – horse reared – still alive – stood watching – stood waited – watched me die – not call help."

Damien's face took on an ashen hue and his voice faltered as he did his best to determine the message. Rosalind staggered backwards until she felt the dining table behind her and yanked out a chair, managing to get it under her only seconds before her legs gave way completely. Her eyes searched the room frantically, searching for something, someone.

"Show yourself Claudia! I need to see your face, I want proof, I need to see your eyes as you tell me…"

"Do you know who this is?" Amelia slipped an arm round her shoulder and positioned herself so the cameraman could get a close up shot of the two women together but Rosalind shrugged her off.

In the editing trailer Charles was now furiously pulling on the door while cursing everyone, both living and dead who could hear him. Unable to escape he turned back to the desk and started randomly hitting buttons trying to stop the filming before two of the crew finally restrained him and pinned in a corner. The man sat at the control desk pressed an extra button and the security camera in the trailer sparked into life, unseen by Charles. After all the man thought, the footage would add an extra dimension and, if his hunch that the man currently wrestling the others, was involved in this revelation, well the footage could be award winning, once court cases were finished.

Back in the dining room, Rosalind was back on her feet pacing back and forth in an attempt to keep Amelia from manhandling her. She turned to Damien,

"I can't see her, or any of them, I sense them, I know when they are near, I can even pick up on their moods, the only time I think I hear them is as I fall asleep and even then I can't be sure but I need to see her, to hear it, from her."

"Everyone form a circle, hold hands. I want you all to focus your energy on the centre of the circle, I call upon on the spirits present to help Claudia appear, help her make herself seen."

Everyone moved into a circle and clasped hands, they waited expectantly, for a few minutes nothing happened then slowly a figure formed. The silence was broken only by the director's voice echoing through the headsets worn by the crew, checking and double checking the cameras were picking up the apparition. Claudia was moving her lips but no sound emanated from her.

"I can see you but I can't hear you, oh Claudia, I can't hear you, please, please, tell me what happened…"

"She doesn't have the strength to make herself seen, and heard, but I have a solution. Not something I normally do, in fact something I prefer to avoid but Claudia I want you to step forward and step into me, use my voice box to communicate."

Damien closed his eyes and they watched in a mixture of fascination, and horror, as the image of Claudia moved and disappeared into the man's body.

His body seemed to expand and contract then the eyes opened once more and fixed on Rosalind.

"Rosa..., Rosal…, Rosalind…"

It took the spirit a few attempts to master working the man's vocal chords and she thought it was a good job she had not been dead longer as she was sure she would have forgotten how to move them completely. Her voice was an octave or two lower than her living voice had been, but she knew Rosalind would know it was her.

"Rosalind, oh my dear, you have no idea how glad I am to get this chance, the chance to tell you what really happened, and I am sorry sweetheart, I really am, but we need you to be safe, as much as we love you, we don't want you joining us, not yet anyway."

"Tell me, tell me it all."

Amelia opened her mouth as if she was going to speak, but realising she might interrupt proceedings she concentrated on looking concerned, hoping the cameraman would remember to keep her in shot.

"I tried to make you hear me so many times, but I just wasn't strong enough, and there are so many things to say but we don't have time now, so just the straight facts of that day, the day your husband killed me."

If it had been a film script, it would have said dramatic pause in the screen directions, but in this case, Rosalind thought, it was more of a brace yourself pause. She felt she should have been more shocked by the revelation that she was, but deep down she suspected she had always known he was capable of anything. Tears swam in her eyes as she cursed herself for her inability to communicate with her spectral relatives directly, and that Claudia was having to go to these lengths to free her.

" I have to be quick I don't have the energy to do this for long. There was a row at breakfast just after you left, he was having a go at the housekeeper over something trivial. I told him it was a sign of him having no class, the way he treated the household staff, he kept calling them servants and I know I should have just walked away but I lost my temper and called him a peasant. I told him half the staff had better breeding than he had and no amount of money could buy him class.

I went to the stables, I had the day planned, spent the morning in the office doing the paperwork, then saddled up Shadow. You remember I was going to enter him into his first eventing show the week after, so I decided to give him an extra run out over the cross country course.

When I got down to where you have to cross the road he was there waiting in the car, I should have just jumped the car, I'm sure Shadow could have managed it but I pulled up instead, he slammed his hand on the horn, Shadow was startled and reared, I held on thought he would just drive off laughing but instead he got out. He had parked so the driver's side was nearest me, the door opening made Shadow back up further, I should have spun the horse round, galloped away but I was furious, I was demanding an explanation of what he was trying to do, I even asked if he was trying to kill me and he stood and laughed.

I didn't realise he had something in his hand until it was too late, he tased the bloody horse, can you believe it, he actually pulled out a Taser and zapped the horse. Shadow reared and then went down, we both went over backwards so I fell and the horse came down on top of me, I couldn't even try to roll clear, my foot was caught in the stirrup."

Claudia seemed to pause but when Damien opened his mouth again it was his own voice which came out.

"She has almost exhausted her energy; she is too weak to talk to you anymore that way. Another lady has stepped forward, the lady from upstairs, she is helping her, but I can finish telling you the story for her, if you will accept it that way."

Amelia began to speak, ready with a dozen questions, but Rosalind held up her hand to silence her, addressing Damien at the same time.

"Yes, please I need to know the rest, but I also need to know if there is any real evidence I am not sure the police will accept the video statement of a ghost."

She smiled as she finished speaking, partly at the idea of the video being shown in court, but also at the knowledge coming over the headphones that the police had indeed been called. She was hearing that Charles had been tied to a chair by the crew in the editing unit, to stop him damaging anything. She rather hoped that he had spoken without thinking, as he so often did, and had incriminated himself.

"Right, let's get on with this, please Claudia is it? Tell Damien the rest, let us hear what happened next."

Amelia moved to stand between Damien and Rosalind, she hoped her interjection would remind the camera man to keep her in shot, but she was talking no chances, and calculated that by standing between them, it would be almost impossible to cut her out of shot.

"I am going to repeat what she tells me, exactly as she says it, okay, let's begin. I was trapped under the horse but I couldn't breathe, I was gasping for breath, I was trying to call to him but he just stood watching, he knew I was alive and he stood and watched as I struggled and begged, he was watching me die and there was nothing I could do.

At one point he got out his phone, I guessed he was ringing you, he was telling you he would be late for lunch, telling you he was having car problems and was just going to stop off at the garage, check the card statements, there will be no garage charges for that day because, as he spoke to you, he was standing watching me die."

Rosalind's hands flew to her face as the truth of her cousin's words came to her. She remembered the call, it had seemed strange at the time as Charles never bothered letting her know if he was going to be late unless they had company, but in the drama of the rest of that day she had forgotten it until now.

"She says the Taser is in the safe in his office, that if it is tested they will find the horses DNA on the prongs. She wants you to know, she was gone by the time the horse came round and got up to return to the stables."

"Why is that important?" Amelia asked softly, her curiosity genuine for the first time that evening.

"Because her foot was still in the stirrup, the horse dragged her back over a mile, it was assumed her injuries were caused by that, even though there were some that seemed inconsistent with being dragged, but no one suspected there was any foul play. I should have known… I should have known…"

Rosalind could take no more and broke down into tears, the camera picked up two pairs of spectral arms wrap themselves round her and a minute later the director called they were done.

An hour later and everything was settling down, Charles had been taken away by the police, and the Taser recovered from his safe. Amelia had recorded her final pieces to camera and been whisked away in a car to her hotel, and the crew had unplugged and wound up any stray wires. Most had returned to the hotel and would come back in the morning to pack up the rest of their stuff.

The director was sat with a policeman in the editing suite, transferring the footage they had collected onto discs, so they could review it, and use what was helpful. Charles had ranted uncontrollably during his imprisonment there, and incriminated himself several times.

An inspector was reassuring the director that it was highly improbable the crew members would be charged with false imprisonment for tying Charles to the chair, and he laughed at the idea of trying to charge a ghost alongside them for holding the door.

Rosalind sat in the drawing room, numb and in shock, Damien passed her a glass, a large measure of brandy reflecting the flames from the fire.

"Here, drink this, it will help you sleep."

"Thanks, I thought you would have gone back to the hotel by now, but I'm glad you stayed back, it helped having a friendly face."

He smiled and sat next to her on the sofa.

"When everything calms down and the dust settles I would like to come back again, if that is okay with you?"

She looked at him quizzically trying to work out the meaning behind his words, for a moment she thought he meant to film more for the show but the look in his eyes dismissed that thought immediately.

"Two motives, one I think you are a really nice person and I would love the chance to get to know you better, and I do mean as friends. I am not going to lie and say I would not be happy if it turned into more than friendship, but I am pretty sure for now, an extra friend can't hurt. If you decide to go ahead with the haunted weekend idea, I can help you there, and for what it is worth, I think it could actually work really well. And the second reason is, I would love the chance to talk to your family, that is, if they decide they will speak to me once there is no film crew there. I think Claudia will, and I hope she can persuade the others that I will be a friend to them, if they let me."

She laughed, the sound seeming strange and inappropriate given the evenings revelations, then becoming serious once more. She looked over to the far end of the room. where she sensed an assortment of ghosts were keeping an eye on her from a respectful distance and allowed another faint smile.

"I think they will oblige, or most will, I would never dare to speak for Sir Henry, and yes, extra friends are always welcome. As for the ghost weekends, I don't know, I will need someone to go through the accounts, I know we still need to find a way to bring in money, I don't know what possessed me to allow Charles to take over running things to the extent I did.

He just never really understood how it all worked. He hated the fact the Claudia was paid an allowance, only twenty thousand a year, but he hated that he could not find a loophole to get out of it. I knew he was greedy but never thought he would resort to… murder. Stupid thing was if he had been a better businessman he would have realised that Claudia's allowance was less than we would have paid someone else to run the stable side of the estate. Her knowledge of horses brought in the money that was keeping us afloat.

The event she was talking about riding the horse in, it wasn't about her competing, she had possible buyers coming to look at the horse, he had real potential, his sale alone would have covered her allowance plus a few months of the stable running costs. We had to destroy him not long after Claudia died, neurological problems. I assumed he had had them before and that was what had caused him to throw her and drag her all that way, or maybe if I am honest, I was glad to have a reason to destroy him. I blamed the poor horse when the person responsible was still sharing my bed."

"You are not to blame for any of this, you could not have known and no one would have blamed you if you had destroyed the horse, medical problems or not, you were upset, you were grieving."

"I know, logically I know what you are saying is true, but right now I feel guilty, feel like I should have known and I can't make it up to Claudia, I can't undo things and bring her back. The only thing that I can do for her, and the others, is find a way to keep the house running, make sure I preserve their home, and this is their home, as much as it is mine, unless of course they decide to move on, but if they go it has to be of their own free will. I don't want any of this cleansing business."

"I would never suggest it, and I am pretty sure this lot would not go, if anyone even tried, but I do think they would help you keep the place running, and intact, and Claudia just whispered that she would be more than happy, to communicate through me, to co-ordinate with you. Right my ride is here, I'll call you in a few days and arrange to come and visit, we can make a start on organising the weekends then if you decide to go ahead with them. Take care of yourself."

As he stood to leave Rosalind noticed it was Damien that blushed and wondered what her cousin had said to him to evoke that reaction. For now, she was exhausted and the only thing she could think of was sleep. After she watched him leave she locked the door and mounted the staircase, in her room she stripped off her clothes and was on the verge of sleep as she fell into the bed, as her eyes closed she thought she heard a voice.

Lady Georgiana leaned over her and placed a kiss on Rosalind's forehead.

"We are so proud of you dearest. Everything will be alright now, we promise."

With that she turned and joined the other spirits stood at the foot of the bed watching over Rosalind. Sir Henry beamed approvingly.

"Could be quite handy having that medium chap around the place, be a lot easier to complain when the damn fool mortals move things without considering the rest of us."

"I should have known you would see it that way, but you never know, in the long run he could be just what she needs, but tonight let her sleep."

Lady Georgiana slipped her arm through Sir Henry's and turning led the rest of the ghosts through the wall and out of the room.

The Shades

She closed her eyes and allowed her head to fall back on to the pillow. Even now the figures danced behind her eyelids, no matter what she did she could not make them fade. Her shift had finished an hour ago, she had eaten the meagre rations they now survived on and wandered into the recreation room only to find it empty. She had decided that if she was going to be forced to remain alone with her thoughts she may as well do it somewhere comfortable, and after returning to her room she had stripped off and lay down on her bunk.

Logically she knew the explanations made sense, chemical reactions creating illusions that the brain sought to make sense of, but she also knew it was a lie. They were real, and they were out there.

The bomb had gone off with only the briefest of notice. She had received the alarm call and dropped everything, speeding to the bunker without paying any attention to the traffic lights or other cars. It was a miracle she had made it here at all, there had been a couple of close calls and she thought with hindsight, she may have caused a few of the collisions she had noticed in her rear view mirror. Any guilt she had felt had been brief, she knew there would be no long term consequences. She had only just made it in time, within minutes of her arrival the sirens had signalled the final shutdown, and all thoughts of those outside had been banished as she took her position.

They had been aware that the threat was real, while civilians had wandered around, their minds full of trivia and petty worries, they, the scientists had been making first contact. She had of course been sworn to secrecy, but she knew that was when the world had changed.

At first countries banded together, sharing information as they tried to fine tune methods of communication with these strange creatures. Then as they had found methods of interacting, ways to understand the patterns of speech, each country had withdrawn and become more secretive, scared to share their discoveries because they did not believe everyone else was giving full disclosure. Looking back at it now it appeared the fears were unjustified, there were not hiding discoveries rather the lack of them, they had all been hiding the fact that they were all getting nowhere fast, they just did not want to be the first to admit it.

She wondered if that had been the creatures plan all along, divide and conquer, let each group believe the others knew something they didn't, some secret that would ultimately give them control.

Now six months later they existed only in isolated pockets, trapped in the very bunkers they believed they were building for our protection.

No one was actually sure who hit the button first.

Everyone had, of course, denied it and no outside observers now existed to prove guilt in any direction.

The final hours of life as she had known it seemed so surreal now looking back. She had no idea that every day actions such as going to the shop would one day take on mythical qualities, how she longed now, to stand in a store, confronted by junk she did not need, that she would never really have needed but desired all the more for its absence.

Deciding what to wear to work had taken an hour each morning, now she rose from her bunk to slip into a clean shirt and trousers, the same outfit as the other three thousand people in this hi-tech prison. That is what it was. They could call it a shelter; they could dress it up in as many fancy names as they like but it would still be a prison. They could not escape, they all wore the same, ate at prescribed times, washed, showered, and slept when they were told. Oh yes, she understood with so many people sharing the limited space and resources, but she did wonder if she had known what it would be like, would she have still climbed into her car and driven here that day.

She had arrived that day and signed into her designated position, she worked in communications and had sat relaying messages between the various stations around the country as they began the final lock downs. Maybe that was part of the reason for her frustrations, since the bomb had blown she had no assigned job. The had not planned for the force of the explosions and subsequent aftershocks destroying the underground fibre optic cables and of course it was impossible for anyone to venture out to fix the problem even if they had known where in the hundreds of miles of cables to begin. She now assisted in any capacity she could, most roles were specialised so she regularly found herself helping with more menial tasks, cleaning and laundry.

She had wondered numerous times as she went about her tasks, which area would suffer from setbacks next, what would happen when machines broke down, would they have the right spare parts or enough parts to last. Occasionally she pondered the organisational skills of those who had planned this base and wondered if they themselves were cocooned somewhere deep in the labyrinth of corridors. It seemed impossible that those who designed and built the shelter would not be here but she knew that was not true, those that had truly built it were not here, that those whose blood and sweat was mixed with the very mortar, they were beneath saving, at least in the opinions of those who made the decisions. The men whose hands had built these walls were out there, dead or… she left the thought unfinished.

She had been working for the agency since leaving university, it had been at her graduation when she had been approached. A nondescript man in a grey suit had handed her his card and suggested she call him, she had almost thrown it away, it had seemed so sleazy at the time and she had been convinced that it was simply a creepy chat up line. Later though, as she had packed up her belongings ready to leave the student accommodation, she had found it tucked into her graduation programme and curiosity had got the better of her.

She had dialled the number ready to hang up the minute he answered but instead it had been a woman who had responded to her hello, she found herself arranging to attend their offices for an interview. After hanging up she had sat staring at the phone, confused by the conversation that had just taken place. She had discovered very little, other than her degree in Media Communications was apparently the qualification they were convinced would make her a perfect candidate for joining their 'agency'. She had questioned the use of that word, expressing that she was not really interested in working in temporary positions however tempting the offer. The woman on the other end of the phone had laughed at that and had said with a tone she could not exactly place 'Miss Adams, I assure you that should you be successful, this will be a position you will occupy for life'.

For life, she'd had no concept of what those two words could mean. She had turned up at what looked like any other office in an affluent area, as she stepped out of the lift taking her to the appropriate floor, her heels had sunk into the plush carpet as she walked across the reception foyer and announced her presence. She had felt so self-conscious as she sank into the leather sofa she had been directed to and waited.

As she had glanced round she had noticed she was not the only candidate, two men and another woman, all of them she guessed in their mid to late thirties, their suits looked designer and she had been suddenly very unsure of her own high street bargain.

She clutched her plastic wallet holding her resume tightly as she looked at the leather wallets and briefcases they all appeared to have with them, she felt like a toddler who had wandered into the big kid's playground. The idea of jumping up and running from the room had been tempting but something had held her fixed in that seat, not for the first time she wondered if she had made the right choice that day.

A siren ripping through the air brought her back to the present. She slowly sat up and swung her legs round, sliding straight into her boots. She could hear footsteps in the corridor, boots moving at speed, but she felt no need to rush to join them, the chances were she would just be in the way.

She grabbed her jacket, pulled it on and tugged the zip up, she did not really need it, the bunker was kept at an ambient temperature, scientifically calculated for maximum efficiency, but returning to your bunk during the day was frowned upon and the jacket hid her crumpled top.

She kept to the edge of the corridor as she headed for her station, which despite the fact it was now more or less redundant was still her point to report to. People were hurrying past her with an urgency she found infectious and she felt her own pace quicken. She slid into her seat and went through the protocol of logging into the system, booting up her console, and announcing her presence ready for duty. She was not prepared for the reply.

"Ah Sarah, nice of you to join us, monitor all wavelengths for any incoming communication, maintain radio silence, do not respond to anything you hear. Understood?"

"Affirmative, scans commencing."

She had replied but at the same time could not help wondering what she was supposed to be listening for, and why now, for months there had been nothing but white noise. Okay she thought, in those first few weeks, she had sat with the headphones on convinced she could make out messages in the static but no amount of enhancing using any programme had made anything legible out of the noise, finally she had accepted it had just been her mind playing tricks.

She turned on more monitors and a row of sound waves sprung to life before her eyes. She knew just from sight that each was recording the wall of static but still she obeyed orders and began the process of listening in to each frequency manually. Like a scanner trying to auto tune a TV she moved up the scale, one wall of noise followed another until her mind began to block out the static, listening in for anything hidden beneath the surface. Once or twice she thought she heard something but when she paused, waiting for any repetition or for any signs of continuity, then there would be nothing, then on she would move to the next frequency.

For hours she repeated the process, knowing that, sat a short distance away from her at both sides, other performed the same task, she did not need to look round to know they were having no more success than she was. She could feel her eyelids growing heavy, lulled by the drone of the sound, the monotony of the endless white noise acting as a lullaby.

She nearly missed it at first. A voice, faint and hard to distinguish, she could not tell if it was a man, woman or a child, nor could she work out what the voice was saying but she knew it was there. She moved on up the frequencies, hoping to refine the quality of the sound, it raced ahead of her, like a feather on the breeze, always just a fraction out of her grasp. Then it was there, quiet but insistent, repeating just one word,

"Come!"

She bit down on her lip, suppressing the urge to reply. She double checked the recording equipment was running before calling her supervisor. No sooner had the final words left her lips than she was surrounded, the five other sound technicians had also picked it up now, they glanced across at each other, trying to show no signs of discomfort as the bustle increased around them. Frantic conversations took place, no directly to them, but around them, before they were manoeuvred towards the door. They were ordered to return to their own quarters and remain there until called to individual debriefings, they were to speak to no one about what they had heard.

Only once she was once more stretched out on the bed did she consider how strange the recent events had been. The whole point of her position was to communicate with any other survivors, but the first signs they find of other life, they act like it is something to be shunned. Still the word choice stood out, *come*, where did they want them to come? Did they want to come here?

Her head was now pounding time to worry later, a few hours' sleep would help, she could only hope that she would be the final one called to discuss what she had heard, after all they had already had a primary report when she notified the supervisor. No sooner than she allowed her eyes to close sleep came, her limbs sunk into the mattress and exhaustion took over.

As she slept the voice came again but it was multiplied, a cacophony of overlapping waves crashing down over her, she could not work out where they were coming from, and could still not distinguish one speaker from another. In her sleep she thrashed, contorting as she sought to escape the intruders in her mind. Her body arched, her hands moved of their own volition, covering her ears as if that would stop the voices inside her head.

Then as suddenly as they started, they ended. The abrupt silence deafened her, and gradually she found her mind was her own once more.

Her personal alarm sounded and she forced her eyes open, exhausted she looked at the clock, it showed hours had passed but her fatigue was greater now than it had been when she had lain down. The bleep of the intercom focused her attention to the fact something was required of her but it took her several minutes to pull herself together enough to physically move.

The debriefing was short, they wanted little more than for her to confirm the information she had provided earlier and back up that general consensus gained from questioning the others, they told her nothing and explained even less. She also kept her secrets, she said nothing of her broken sleep, what would she say, really, I dreamt I heard voices in my sleep? They would say she imagined it, but she knew that were not true and that there was more to it. There had been a single voice over the airwaves, but in her mind there had been dozens, she had begun to catch a hint of different voices, individual tones.

It was the multitude that had called out to her in her sleep. That meant something, she was sure of it, over the airwaves the single voice had been unclear but the voices in her head, they had left her in no doubt what they wanted. They wanted her, they wanted her to go to them, to join them. She had no idea if she was the only one they had singled out or whether the others who had heard the lone voice were also experiencing the same dreams as they took their turns to lie down and close their eyes.

Weeks passed and the voices became frequent visitors, both over the airwaves and in her dreams but that had not been the only development. There had been movement on the screens, at first it looked like smoke or mist, then shadows appearing to move within the swirling grey tendrils but nothing you could identify or define. If only it had stayed that way she thought to herself.

She desired sleep but had become reluctant to return to her bed, she knew the voices would hound her, despite the heaviness of her eyelids she resisted, it was a month since she had heard that first voice and she knew from the dark circles round the eyes of ours she was not alone. She had just finished a six-hour stint, they no longer wore the headphones and listened to the voices rather they watched the sound wave graphics watching for any anomalies, there had been none.

She headed to the cafeteria, though she did not desire human interaction the presence of others was a comfort. People sat around, divided by their department, everyone was subdued, if a pin had dropped, it would have deafened the room.

A few people looked towards her, no one made any attempt to engage her or motion for her to join their tables. She grabbed a tray and moved along the service table trying not to pay too much attention to what was slopped onto her tray, highly nutritious and almost taste free was the way it was usually described. She took a seat and proceeded to stir the brown porridge like meal round her plate and allowed her mind to wander.

As the figures outside had begun to take on a clearer form she had noticed those of them on the inside had stopped making eye contact with each other. No one wanted to be caught thinking the same as the person next to them, while it was just your own belief it was easier to try to cling on to the false explanations you were given, but once you acknowledged that others shared those thoughts and doubts, then that became dangerous.

Several people had disappeared after speaking out, openly challenging the lie that the figures before them were only illusions. How could illusions take the form of people they knew? Not just those that people had been close to, relatives and loved ones that you might expect the mind to conjure up, but others, people from the peripheries of people's lives?

One man had been sedated as he screamed about having seen the man from his local paper shop, the man who had served him his paper and cigarettes en-route to work each morning for twenty years, back before the bomb had gone off. He had argued if it had been his imagination he would have wished his wife or children into existence, not a man he had barely spoken to as he handed him a five pound note and received change from with a nod.

After that there had been another round of meeting, then a lecture series explaining the illogicality of the hallucinations, how while the conscious mind may think of one person, subconsciously simple things like daily routines could be influencing factors.

She carried on pushing the food round her tray, the voices were getting louder each time she heard them, they were growing clearer, louder and more insistent. And it was not just the voices she thought, the images themselves had at first been mere shadows, grey and indistinct, now…

She dropped her fork and it clattered loudly against the tray, she glanced round to see if she had drawn unwanted attention to herself but everyone stared down at their own trays determined to resist the urge to look despite any well-hidden curiosity.

She let her mind draft back to her own thoughts, whatever they were they were not flesh and blood, not human certainly. Gradually they had become more distinctive, clothes and vague features had begun to form, people claiming to recognise them as people, though she herself had witnessed that at the minute it was only individual people who saw them clearly, anyone else staring at the same shape saw only the general appearance of a person. The last few days it had seemed as if some were getting stronger, appearing more solid, as if the becoming... but becoming what?

She could not get her thoughts straight, nothing made sense and once more she wished she could simply believe the lies.

It was at that moment a scream tore through the silence.

She had turned her head and was staring before she even realised she had reacted, but she noticed she was not the only one. A young woman was stood in the middle of the cafeteria, hands clutched claw like over her ears. To those who had not experienced it, it looked like she was trying to block out her own voice, but Sarah knew better, she had felt close to doing the same several times, and could not help but wonder what had been the final straw to push this woman over the edge. She did not have to wait long to find out.

The woman's companions were seeking to control her now, and force her to settle back into her seat, another woman in a supervisor's uniform delivered a resounding slap to the hysterical woman's cheek. A red hand print flamed against the deathly pale skin, but it achieved the desired effect and the screaming ceased abruptly. The woman looked about frantically and words began to issue from her mouth incoherently. Slowly, as she was coaxed into sitting and implored to calm herself, the words began to form partial sentences. From the fragments Sarah could overhear she began to piece the woman's story together.

The woman worked monitoring the screens, as Sarah had listened to the voices become stronger this woman had watched them emerge from the fog, shadows taking shapes then becoming shades.

That was how many people described them and Sarah knew it was a description that fitted, looking at them was like watching a person stood in the shade, they looked like themselves but you could not make out all the details. For this woman the shades had just been visual at first but the voices had begun a few days ago. It seemed she like so many of them had coped initially, trusting the agency explanation, for her it made sense, the more attention you paid to something the more your mind would rationalise it.

The woman was now trying to explain the building pressure, the way the voices had become clearer as the shades had gained more features. Sarah could tell from the furtive glances passing between the others she and the woman were not the only ones who had been hearing an increasing number of voices. The woman had stilled and in a quiet voice the final straw was revealed.

"It was my sister, I thought I saw her before but now I know it was her, I heard her voice, she called my name. She is out there and she is waiting for me, she was calling to me, she was crying!"

The woman now broke down completely, heavy sobs racked her body, Sarah wondered how she would cope if she heard the voice of someone she knew, but for her there was no one out there to haunt her, her loved ones were ghosts long before the alarm had gone off.

The woman was being led from the room, the movement of her shoulders showed she was still fighting to regain her composure and losing the battle. Sarah pushed the tray away, she could not even pretend she had an interest in food now, her only hope was that she was so tired now sleep might come without bringing the voices.

It was two weeks later when the announcement came over the loudspeakers calling them all to the conference hall. Sarah left her room and was immediately caught up in a sea of bodies all moving in the same direction, she allowed herself to be carried along in the tide of people. As she moved along a tidal wave of whispers crashed over her as everyone speculated on this unusually summoning, no one seemed to have known it was coming nor had any idea what they were about to hear.

Upon reaching the conference hall she was shocked to see that when they had called for all personnel to attend they had meant it literally. The hall was designed to seat around three hundred people but now over four times that number was crammed in doing their best to find a position that allowed them to see the platform that had been erected at the far end of the room. Stood upon the dais were all the directors and department heads but also a few people she did not recognise but knew to be the decision makers who had shut themselves away in a private wing ever since the lock down had begun leaving the supervisors to see to the normal ever day running of the place.

On the wall behind them they had mounted a huge screen and as more people tried to manoeuvre themselves into a prime viewing position Sarah struggled to keep the stage in sight, finally in the interests of self-preservation she edged to the back corner deciding that she would rather watch the screen than be crushed in the throng.

The director of the agency was calling for silence, she recognised him despite only having met him once before, the day after lock down, but he had featured in several of the training videos, though he had looked distinctly younger on those. He had begun by discussing recent events, the way the shades had developed and what he believed the consequences were. She struggled to keep up with him, as he spoke his speech became filled with technical terms, and an uneasy feeling came over her.

Finally, he gestured towards the screen and it flickered to life, figures clutching flowers appeared. it took her a minute to realise what she was looking at, it was an external feed, the shades now looked solid, many stood huddled and appeared to be crying, exclamations rung out round the room as people spotted those they knew. The director motioned again and the screen went blank.

He was no explaining that they were responsible for this, it was their emotions which were stopping them from resting in peace, summoning them back through grief. They were creating this illusion, and so, for the good of everyone, they would cease all outside monitoring for the foreseeable future. Anyone who continued to hear any voices should report to medical where they would be prescribed medication to help block these hallucinations. Those with jobs such as Sarah's would be reassigned for the time being,

He was now seeking to reassure them all that the doctors and scientists were in complete agreement that with the removal of stimulus these shades would disappear, it was merely a matter of time, and then normal assignments could be resumed. They just had to put all thoughts of their past lives out of their minds, it was that simple.

It was the explanation everyone would cling to; the shades were a mass hallucination brought on by the guilt of leaving loved ones behind on the surface when they had been saved. Survivor guilt. Grief and guilt had fed the emotions and brought the situation to a head, that was all.

Sarah and the others filed out of the room and headed back towards their own rooms or departments for those on duty. A palpable relief at a rational explanation flowed from the majority of people. She could see a few still struggling to accept it but, what was the alternative she thought, it was either a hallucination or ghosts, either was the only thing she hoped was that they could silence the voices for good.

One hundred and fifty metres above the curtain swished back to reveal the shining new plaque. It was positioned next to a bricked up doorway. Engraved in a stylish font a simple memorial to the 1547 people who had died trapped below ground during a tragic accident twelve months previously.

The public had not been told the truth of course, of the obscure agency running a covert simulation which had gone horribly wrong, how the people underground had died believing that they were the ones about to survive a nuclear attack. A dropped vial of a biochemical they were developing had triggered a lock down, the building had been sealed immediately and the computer system had taken control.

It had shut the whole complex down, the system had worked too well and not allowed any form of manual override. Rescue had been impossible, those trapped below had died slowly as life support shut down and the oxygen ran out. There had been no survivors.

Voices Across The Void

The man in the grey suit stood at the rear of the crowds, and waited until they slowly drifted away in two's and three's until finally he stood alone.

Next time, he thought, he wondered if any of them knew the cover story of alien contact, if anyone of those who lives had been lost had weakened over a glass of wine, but surely if they had it would have come out by now. No, they were in the clear, compensation had been paid out where needed, it was almost time to meet the minister.

He bowed his head for a moment before turning and walking towards the large town car awaiting him, next time…

THE ELEVATOR

It had not been a good day, Priscilla stood tapping her finger against her arm as she waited while the elevator stalled on the floor above. The only thing on her mind was the prospect of a warm bath and a chilled glass of wine when she got home. She wanted to push this place and everything connected to it out of her mind until tomorrow. She would deal with the unsatisfied clients in the morning, grovelling and apologizing for her colleague's incompetence.

A grinding of gears announced the elevator was moving once again, she shifted her weight as she tried to ease the aching in her feet from an afternoon of rushing round in heels. A bell announced its arrival, the doors slid apart and she stepped in glancing round at the only other occupant, who stood staring ahead of him, seeming not to notice her entrance.

She turned to face the door, the man seemed in a world of his own as the doors closed and they began to descend. Standing a little behind him, she allowed her eyes to study him. She knew only his first name, Tyler, and that he worked for the accounts department on the floor above. The girls in the office all swooned when he was required to come down a floor in search of missing paperwork, at times she suspected that files were deliberately mislaid to ensure his presence when things were quiet.

She could not deny his looks, he was the quintessential tall, dark, and handsome hero young girls were taught to desire, but she herself had never paid him much attention. Romance and work were not a healthy combination she preferred her business and private lives to be separate. Her eyes skimmed across his back noticing the way his suit was taut against the clearly defined muscles of his shoulders and back, if she ever were to mix business and pleasure she mused, he would be a good candidate for it to happen with.

She looked across at the panel showing the floors as they passed, the elevator seemed to be going very slowly today, only two floors had passed as she had been observing him. As if aware of her thoughts he turned and smiled

"It has been going slow all day."

She forced a smile back, trying not to let it show, that his smile and, a spark in his deep blue eyes, had affected her.

Unconsciously, her hand strayed to the chain around her throat, and she toyed with the locket that hung there. A present from her ex, with whom she had shared a home, and an office, until she found out she also shared a secretary, or to be more accurate, he was borrowing her secretary for more than note taking. It had been six months since she packed his bags and quit her job, she had been lucky to walk straight into this one. The locket was a reminder to her to keep her guard up, she would not allow herself to be hurt that way again.

She found her eyes drawn back to him. She watched the way his dark hair brushed against the collar of his shirt, and despite her best efforts, could not help but wonder, how it would feel to allow her hands to follow the contours down from his neck, towards his waist, to nestle into him and brush her lips against the hollow of his collarbone.

A loud thud and the lurch of the elevator jerking to an abrupt halt brought her out of her daydream.

As the elevator halted Priscilla lost her balance, the heels that she wore as part of her daily corporate uniform failed her, sending her forward through the air. Instinctively she reached out, grasping Tyler's arm to steady herself, as soon as she regained her equilibrium she pulled her hand back, as if the cloth of his suit had burnt her hand.

"Sorry!" She found herself apologizing, despite the fact he had turned to her and smiled.

"Not a problem, are you okay?"

"Yes, it just caught me off guard, I just hope it isn't stuck for too long."

She reached out her hand to the control panel, hitting each button, hoping that it would spur the elevator to movement. She reached finally for the alarm button, pressing it several times, before a voice crackled into the intercom, explaining there was a power cut, an accident in the street, a car had hit something, it would be back up as soon as the engineer arrived.

She stepped back aware there was nothing they could do but sit back, and wait. She looked around at the steel walls, wondering how long she would be able to bear being in here. Tyler seemed to sense her unease, and turned to face her, loosening his tie, he began complaining he would not make the ball game he was heading to that evening if they were held up long. She was aware he was trying to pass the time, and distract her from the fact they could be trapped for hours, but as he spoke she found herself drifting off, contemplating what it would be like to feel his lips against hers.

She made the effort to return his conversation, all the time taking in each of his features, the lines that appeared round the corner of his eyes when he smiled, made her realize he was, perhaps, a few years older than she had believed previously. She had thought him in his mid-twenties, too young to consider for anything more than a fling, not that she would have considered having one, she quickly reminded herself.

She was becoming aware of the walls closing in on her, she could feel herself growing warm, and feel her heart pounding in her chest. She felt it was beating so loudly surely he must hear it, she slipped her jacket from her shoulders, her eyes now leaving him and flitting round looking for an escape route from the shrinking metal cage which encased them. His words were muted now as if they were coming to her through water, she could see concern spread across his face, and his arm reaching for her. She felt herself falling, then dull pain as she met the floor, before everything went dark.

In the darkness, she saw streams of blood running down the elevator walls, she ran between them, pounding on the cold hard metal as she screamed for help. She knew she was not alone, a figure stood watching her. It did not move or speak, just stood watching, she flew at it now, pounding her fists against the unyielding flesh. She felt strong hands grasp her wrists, holding her, restricting her movement as she sought to drive the figure away from her.

A voice was speaking to her, pleading tones penetrated her hearing yet the words themselves remained indistinct. She could hear her own blood as it raced through her body, her heart racing as fear tore through her. She was trapped here with the dark figure, again she renewed her struggles, she could feel the walls closing in on her.

Frantically she pushed the figure away, and backed up, only to realize too late, she had placed herself in the corner, and escape was now cut off. Her hands reached along the walls clawing for a weapon, something to drive this spectral being away, but finding only sleek smooth steel beneath her fingertips. Again it advanced towards her, making soothing noises, she had no choice but to go on the offensive, and she flew towards him, swinging her arms wildly hoping to knock it off guard and allow her escape.

She saw the arm raise, but could not avoid the blow which made contact with her cheek. The sting of the palm contacting her cheek stunned her, the force of the blow knocking her backwards, banging her head against the wall behind her. Her senses overwhelmed, the blackness came again and her eyes closed.

When she come round again, she was aware of the proximity of Tyler as he held her arms against her side. Concern was etched in his eyes, but it was the mark on his cheek, which caught her attention.

"Did I do that?"

The tremor in her voice a mixture of fear of the situation, and shame, that she should have caused the swelling welt that stood angrily upon his previously perfect skin.

"You were scared, you didn't recognize me. I have been hit harder, not much I admit but no lasting harm done."

His voice had a musical quality to it now as he replied, a smile playing enticingly across his lips. She wondered what it would be like to feel those lips against hers, he was so close she could feel his breath brush against her.

Then he was standing, helping her to her feet. She brushed down her skirt, and adjusted herself trying to regain her composure. She felt silly worrying about how she looked given the way she had just acted, but she could not help it, suddenly his opinion of her mattered. She turned away from him so he would not see her face as she began to explain the reason for her reaction.

She told him briefly of her childhood, the stepfather who locked her in the cupboard when she was bad, which in his opinion, was a daily occurrence. She found the words pouring from her lips, about the string of failed relationships, where she had allowed herself to be treated in abusive ways, ways that left her drawing further away from intimacy.

She told him of how work had always been her way to escape life, both mentally, and of her need for financial independence, which had allowed her to escape each relationship once it turned bad. At the outset of every new love affair she knew, expected, it would go bad in the end

. He remained silent as the words flowed out, filling the space around her, pushing the walls back. In speaking so openly, for the first time with someone other than the expensive therapists she had confided in, it was as if she were setting her past free, ready to leave it behind and a weight lifted from her. Finally, she was done, with a deep breath she turned to face him, unaware he now stood right behind her.

As she turned his lips met hers softly, savouring the moment, and she did not resist. Instead she yielded to him, her body melting against his. He pulled his lips away, his hand reaching up, fingertips tracing her cheekbone, pushing her hair back from the slender neck as he told her how long he had wanted this. His confessions now mingled with her words, filling the void between them, the deliberately misplaced paperwork that he used as an excuse to come down a floor, the calls where she picked up her phone but he lost his nerve pausing long enough to hear her voice before replacing the handset. He understood she did not mix work and pleasure, he was changing jobs next week, there would no longer be a conflict for her.

Now it was she who reached forward touching the mark on his face, once more apologizing, before his lips silenced her. This time, the gentle pressure he had applied before, was replaced by an urgency which surprised her, yet she felt herself responding to him. Her hands reached up, fingers burying themselves into his hair, pulling him closer. Now his hands moved across her body tracing the outline of her breasts through the silk blouse, she longed for him to slide his hands beneath the soft material, to feel the flesh on flesh contact her body was crying out for. Hands moved now, skimmed over her curves, as if mapping her body for further exploration at a later date. She allowed her own hands to trace the contours of his back that she had admired earlier, moving down to his taut muscular buttocks. She felt her arousal growing, despite the fact no actual skin contact had been made, other than that of their lips, which were still locked together. A voice in her head told her still it was madness, but she silenced it with the brush of her hand across the bulge forming in his trousers, a gasp escaped her lips, as a low moan slid from his.

In a moment of madness, she thought about what it would be like to drop to her knees, there and then, and take him into her mouth, to forget where they were, and the risk of being caught. She flushed at the images that drifted into her mind, his lips drawing her nipple into his mouth, their limbs twisted into impossible positions, making it so you could not tell where one person ended and the other began. These thoughts could not be hers, her eyes opened a fraction to see him staring at her, and knew somehow these were his thoughts she was sharing, the mental symbiosis sent a fire spreading through her body, and she dug her fingers into his back, drawing him closer still.

A shudder startled her, it took a few seconds for her to process the fact the elevator had once more resumed its descent. She pulled her had back as if her fingers had been burnt, Tyler seemed unaware of the change, and was reluctant to allow her to pull back from him. She could not fail to notice the longing in his eyes as she stepped back from him.

Giggling like a naughty child she smoothed down her clothes once more and shook her hair out trying to release the tangles caused by their embrace. She knew she was smiling, that as soon as the door opened, anyone seeing her would know a change had taken place in her. Three floors to go she leaned in and placed another quick kiss upon his lips tenderly, she did not notice he had not bothered straighten his shirt. She did not notice the sadness mingled in with the longing in his eyes

They were nearly down now, she faced the doors and composed herself, she knew she had said no more office romances but she could not just ignore what had happened, she had just told him more of her past than she had most of the people in her life. Maybe, she could suggest they take it slow, but she could ask him for a drink, or for dinner, then she could explain more, they could take it from there. Yes, that was the way to go.

As the elevator shuddered to a halt she turned back to him before the doors opened and he walked out, but she was alone.

She spun round, the elevator was empty, the doors opened but the foyer in front of her was also devoid of any signs of life. It didn't make sense. She had not been dreaming, it had been real she knew it had but she could think of no explanation. She needed to get out of here, needed fresh air, panic swelled in her, could she have imagined it but if she hadn't where could he have gone, people can't just disappear she told herself.

As she reached the doorway she noticed a crowd of people, they seemed stunned, in shock, an ambulance had pulled up and as the paramedics moved the crowd back she saw him through the gap their arrival had created.

There, laying on the floor, was Tyler, her first reaction was that in his haste to get away from her he had run our straight into traffic, but she knew that was not possible.

She approached the crowd asking if anyone knew what had happened, several explained he had been coming out of work and the car that hit him had lost control and mounted the pavement. It had been quick, he had no time to move, it had started a chain reaction that led a minute or two later to another car swerving to avoid the incident had collided with the traffic lights and shorted out the electrics in the street.

As the debates began between witnesses, to the exact way he was hit, the reasons for the accident she had walked forward, in a trance like state she tried to work out what was happening.

It was like being in a dream she could not wake from, she could see the paramedics working on him, paddles attached, trying to jolt him back to life.

Then across the street she saw him, he was watching her, he stood, cars passing through him and he gazed at her. Was he waiting? Did he want something from her?

She was confused, her emotions chasing each other through her consciousness, she had decided to give him a chance but now it seemed like it had been taken away, if she asked him would he return to his body, could he return? What if she asked him and he refused? It seemed ridiculous but she was not sure she could handle that rejection, but what if she didn't ask and he stayed dead, would that be her fault? Could she live with herself, if he didn't live?

She returned his stare, she thought about shouting to him but it came to her that if she could see him like this when no one else could, maybe she just had to think it for him to know. *Please, please, come back, give us a chance to see what will happen. No promises, but I want to try, I need to try.*

He must have heard her and understood, because he smiled and she watched as he approached his body, he never took his eyes from hers, until that last moment, when he disappeared back into the flesh.

His body jumped and the current passed through it but this time a breath escaped his lips with an audible gasp. His hand reached out to her and she moved forward and clasped it. As the paramedic worked readying him for the trip to hospital she knelt by his side holding his hand, his anchor to this life.

She wondered how much he would remember of his out of body experience and how it could have felt so real, and she could not help but wonder, if he could make her feel so alive as a ghost, then how would he make her feel when she finally was in his flesh and blood arms.

THE HOSPITAL

I should not be here!

I was supposed to go, but you held me here, now I am waiting for you. I saw the light so warm and inviting, beyond it the most wonderful garden that I longed to step forward into. I tried to move forward, but your love held me, I was not bitter, just incredibly sad as the light faded and I remained.

I look over at you from where I stand in the corner of the room as you sit by the bed clinging to the shell which lies there. You speak so softly, so lovingly, to the body which I used to inhabit.

I try to move away to walk from the room, at the doorway I meet resistance and can move no further, if I push against it, I can force my head through the door to look at the corridor beyond. Out there, life continues, people rush to and fro, some living, some like me trapped here. Neither the living nor dead, pay me any heed as I withdraw back to your vigil by my bedside. I move behind you as you lean against the bed your head grazing against the thin sheets that you have pulled right up to my neck, in an attempt to hide the tangle of wires that monitor and sustain.

I can hear your sobs and your pleas, but I cannot fulfil your request and return to you, the body you hold is too badly damaged for me to re-enter it.

It is strange, I look at myself, or rather, the body which held me, contained me, and I feel nothing, no emotion attached to it or to its loss. I think of all the wasted time I spent worrying about getting it in shape, keeping it trim, preening, plucking, bronzing and for what? So that when my final journey began I could look down at it, observing how a few seconds could change it beyond recognition, and that in the end understand, ultimately, it meant nothing.

I remember when we first met we were both young and care free, I want to reach out and touch your face. I want to let my fingers trace the contours of a thousand tiny lines created by the tears and laughter of a long and happy life. I want so badly to wipe away the tears that run in rivulets between the wrinkles that line your cheeks.

I remember when you first asked me out, you were so hesitant, expecting rejection but daring to ask anyway, how I loved you for that, now as I look at you, I see that same look in your eyes, the longing mixed with resignation. I wish I could make this easier for you, take away the pain and soothe your fears, as you have mine down the years.

Activity in the doorway draws my attention, the children have arrived.

Our daughter bursts into the room, as always too much energy to be contained within her, manifesting itself in a whirlwind that seems to accompany her every movement. I watch helpless as she fires question after question at you, not allowing you time to answer, though if she did allow it, it would be worse for all at this time. They would not be the answers she would want to hear, and it would take away her ability to deny what she knows in her heart.

Our son follows, a few minutes behind, he of course has taken the time to gather the facts from the staff, he looks at you and for a moment, I fear for you that he will confront you, but he does not, it is almost as if he senses that to do so would start a chain reaction which can never be stopped.

The doctor now joins you all, the small room is filled with life and grief, I feel the outsider surrounded by my own family and though I know I no longer take up any space, I back up into the corner making myself smaller.

The doctor is once again explaining that what they can see, the signs of life, breathing and a pulse, are false, created only by machines. You shake your head, refusing to accept it, our daughter now dramatically throws herself down to her knees, clutching the hand that you hold, she is begging you to see sense and turn the machines off, the more she pleads the more you resist. Her brother pulls her away calming her, as he has so many times down the years.

It is a strange relationship they share, polar opposites, yet the bond of twins tying them to each other in some inexplicable way that even we struggled to understand. Ours, in some ways, was a house of opposites, you and I and the twins, two pairs that understood and complimented each other perfectly yet to the outside world appeared strange combinations.

It is his turn to try to reason with you now, he is so much like you, quiet, patient and so calm, few others could see the other qualities you share, the fierce protectiveness and deep passions which burn hidden deep inside. He challenges you, turn the machines off, see what happens, if I am there then I won't stop breathing. Of course he knows I am no longer there, and he knows, deep down, so do you. You don't look at him, just shake your head, daring him silently to say what is on all your minds.

It wasn't your fault. I know it and so do you. And once they hear all the facts, have time to consider everything, they will know it too. They had been questioning whether you should still be driving for months, we all had. Maybe they were right in that your reaction times were slower since the stroke, but, if everyone drove as well as you, there would never have been an issue. Even if you had been at your fastest, you could not have stopped what happened, you could not have stopped a teenager in a stolen car pulling straight out in front of you.

There was nowhere else to go, no avoiding the impact, they told you that it was a miracle you had survived, as if that should give you comfort, instead I know it only adds to your pain. You think you should be with me, or have traded places at the very least.

All those travelling in the other car were killed, the two in front against the dashboard and windscreen, killed in their seats, and the one sat in the rear, killed me. Part of me is glad, that is unfair of me and I don't really feel anger towards them but there is bitterness. Yes, there is definitely bitterness that their actions brought us all here, that their choices squander the precious lives we all held, and caused pain to those who love us all. Maybe I realised more than they ever could have, that their families will suffer just as you do.

The boy in the back was not wearing a seatbelt, when the cars collided he flew in the air, the bonnet had already crumpled as the vehicles melded into one. As he flew out one windscreen he slammed into the other, shattering it, a thousand diamond like fragments filled my lap before he followed. I was slammed back into my seat, ribs crushed and punctured, other internal organs lacerated.

Looking down now I can see the myriad of tiny scratches covering my face and neck where the glass showered down on me, wounds that will never become scars. A random thought passes through my mind about how much make up it will take to cover them. My friends and I had joked about those who wore their make up like camouflage, trying to hide the years, and I hope that you will opt for a closed casket and spare me that final embarrassment.

I laugh and my hand flies to my mouth, then I freeze, at first scared I will have been heard, I was always one to be guilty of inappropriate responses, then I realise, not only can you not hear me, but the sound did not even come from my mouth. I know I retain a shadow of the physical body I have spent so many years living in, but I am becoming aware that I am not restricted by it any longer, I am so much more.

The doctor has left and the three of you sit, surrounding the bed in an uneasy silence. Our daughter fidgeting in her seat, unable to keep still. You, with tears still flowing, eyes fixed on mine, desperate for a sign of life, and our son, I know mentally he is compiling a checklist of phone calls to be made, people to be notified, things which must be done. Of all of you he is the one I worry about least, he will not show his grief publically but he will do it privately while maintaining the calm exterior required to deal with the formalities.

I know you will fall apart, for a while at least, and out daughter will become mother to the man who bounced her on his knee. I also know the strain this will place upon your relationship, you will not appreciate her fussing and clucking, and she will do it all the more, trying to make things right and compensate, all while avoiding dealing with her own feelings. I know all this and am powerless to make it different, and I know how it will be, because I know your natures, and things can be no other way.

I realise I am viewing the scene with detachment, that is not to say I do not love you all as much as I did before the world was ripped away, but that a serenity has settled upon me. I can see it all and feel the love radiating within the room, reminiscent of the way the sun's rays warmed the kitchen each morning as I boiled the kettle for the first coffee of the day.

I am content, and I know I should feel guilty for these feelings when you are all hurting so badly, but I know you would not want me to share your pain.

More doctors come and there is much discussion in hushed tones, I can guess what has happened from your reaction, when we signed the donor register I don't think either of us really considered they would find anything usable by the time old age had ravaged us, though if I am honest I am shocked they can find anything useful now.

I know they have asked the question, I feel angry on your behalf, I understand time is of the essence but they know you have not yet accepted my loss. Maybe they thought this would bring it home to you, but you are vehement in your protests and out son calms the storm once more.

I know he is telling them that you need more time, and that as a family they of course want to follow my wishes, but they need to understand more time is needed, always more time, the one thing I no longer have.

More is said in whispers, directly to our son so that you do not hear, but I watch his face drain as the realisation of the true situation hits him. They cannot just turn off the machines and leave me to go and allow you to stay by my side. The minute I flat line, the organs must be harvested for the best chance of success, no lingering goodbyes for us, cold clinical realities must take precedence.

My son is torn between two parents now, how to respect the wishes of one while allowing the other the closure they need. How I long to wrap my arm around my boy, he has moved and stands now by the door, looking over at where you sit by my side, and he looks so small and defeated, like a child once more, my child who needs me, though I know he would never admit it.

I see the shutters come down behind his eyes, his defence mechanism that makes him the one strong enough to face what is to come. He announces that they should leave, he and his sister, that they will allow you a few hours alone with me, and that when they return, they will discuss what is to be done. For a moment I think you will argue, demand an explanation of his words, but I see the resignation in your eyes, though in your heart you do not believe you can be persuaded, could never accept defeat so easily.

Our daughter presses her lips to your cheek, and her tears leave a trail down your face as they mingle with yours, next, a stiff, awkward embrace with our son, neither of you comfortable with each other.

Then they leave, and the walls you were fighting so hard to preserve come crashing down, you collapse on the bed, clutching at the hand nearest you, desperately squeezing, hoping for a response that cannot come. For one brief minute I do consider it, I try to draw near to the body which I so recently left, but already I can smell the beginning of decay. A sickly sweet smell as the flesh yields to death, and I know there is no returning.

I want to reach out and comfort you, as I try my hands pass through you and for a fleeting moment you shudder and I believe you felt me. I cannot stand and watch you in pain, unable to give solace or comfort. I looked round like an animal cornered, searching for escape, before I know it, I am out in the corridor.

I have no concept of movement, I merely wished to be gone from the room and I was. This is a new development, and I marvel at the speed with which these new experiences are happening, earlier it had required effort to just reach the door, and I had moved as if I was still limited by the flesh. Now I begin to understand that the only thing holding me back is, what would previously have been known as, my imagination.

I am beginning to realise the freedom I have now, without the cumbersome body restricting me, though I am not totally free. Like a child in the womb I am tethered to my flesh by an invisible umbilical cord, it binds me but it is not my flesh that nourishes it, rather it is you, or more correctly your love, which feeds it and holds me in place.

I look round now and see I am not alone. The corridor is filled with the living, they dash back and forth, salvaging the damaged, patching them up, repairing the fragile bodies as best they can. It strikes me suddenly, I had never thought of the body as so easily broken before, I had always thought of it in terms of its resilience and healing abilities, as a vessel for giving life not one emptied of it. But, before I have chance to dwell on this, it is the dead who demand my attention.

They pass amongst the living, as different in death as they were in life. Some wander lost, seemingly unaware of where they are or what has become of them. Others bluster and rush round, I notice the shivers of the living as these spirits pass by.

I consider the choice of word, is that what I am now, a spirit, or a ghost? Is there a difference? When the bond to the flesh is finally severed and I can leave, will I be able to return? Will I be able to watch over you? Or will I be trapped here wandering these corridors? Questions suddenly overwhelm me and a sense of panic descends.

I turn away from these others, as if by banishing them from my sight my worries will disappear alongside them, but the anxiety continues to build.

Then I see her.

Her smile lights up her face just as I remember, and though she looks younger than I ever saw her, I am calmed by her presence.

My mother embraces me, though the word does not really convey the action, or the depth of the moment. She has come to wait with me, to take me home with her when the time comes, and help me adjust to this new reality. I realise that I no longer need to ask questions, a simple thought is enough to bring total understanding.

Calmed now by my mother's presence, I can begin to truly appreciate the situation I am in. I watch as others appear, whether they have just passed, or it is that I have only just become aware of them, I cannot be sure but it does not matter, the probability is that it is a mix of both. Some seek out the living, frantically trying to gain their attention and occasionally, very occasionally succeeding.

There is a woman, probably about my own age, she looks directly at me and smiles, I look round behind me to see who else the smile could be aimed at but behind me is just blank wall. My mother smiles back at me and nods, before explaining to me that there really are those who can see and communicate with spirits, I feel something akin to guilt, for all the times I dismissed all who made such claims as charlatans.

A small child wanders in and approaches a young couple sat nervously fidgeting in the corner. They pay the child no attention, and I am indignant for her before it becomes clear they cannot see her. The child is crying now, my heart is breaking for her, I cannot imagine the confusion the child must be feeling, unable to comprehend what is happening. I instinctively move forward to go to her but my own mother holds me back.

Just as I am about to protest a woman appears next to the child, and older woman, I assume a grandmother, and she hurries the child away, back the way she came, my mother whispers that it was not her time yet.

A short while later, a man in scrubs approached them, the surgeon, I guessed, concern, pain, then relief all show on their faces as he recounts their neat loss. I wish there was a way to give my family the same relief, but that is beyond science as much as it is beyond their prayers.

We wander around the hospital, I have no idea of the passing of time in conventional terms, but I do know that morning is approaching by the red glow of sunrise on the horizon, I know this is the last I will see from this side. I have a great desire to be by your side for the start of this final day of our life together, well, this chapter of our life at least, I have no doubt, when your time comes, I shall be allowed to return to greet you.

When I enter the room you are asleep with your head on the bed, your eyes are still puffy from the tears, but other than that, you look at peace, and I hate that you will have to awake to the pain once again.

My mother, who has always loved you like a son, approaches you and lays her hand on your forehead, you seem to stir a little in your sleep, and a smile half forms on your lips, giving away the fact she has just communicated with you in some way. It is her way of showing me how I can say my goodbye.

I step forward now and take her place, but rather than a hand, it is my lips I press to your warm flesh, wishing I could kiss away the frown lines that have embedded themselves over the last few hours.

Then we are together, stood at home in our garden, bathed in the sun as it rises over the trees. We are telling each other everything we know but never express, how much we love each other, how good the life we had was. I am telling you that it is okay to let me go, that I need you to do it for both our sakes. I tell you I will be waiting, I will always be waiting, but there is no rush, time means nothing to me, I only need to know he will go on until it is his time, that he must not try to find me before then. I feel a weight lift from you, I know now you can face what you must do.

The garden fades as you open your eyes, and look around you, you look towards where I lay and smile, then I stand beside you as you pick up your mobile and text the children to return as soon as they can.

It is only a little while later when they both rush in. They are worried by your message, and have spoken to each other already, they had expected to find some change in my condition upon their arrival and are confused that nothing has changed.

You explain your dream to them, our meeting in the garden, though you keep much of it to yourself. You allow them time to process what you are saying, reassure them you can handle this now, before you call for the doctors and tell them it is time.

Forms are placed in front of you and you sign them, not without hesitation, but you look out at the sunshine, and write your name on the lines marked with crosses. Then the doctor, assisted by two nurses, removes first the drips, then the monitors, and finally the tubes from down my throat.

Then the nurses leave and the doctor steps back to allow you to say your goodbyes before he steps back into action.

One by one you step forward, you each press your lips against my pale face, you hold my hands looking for a sign of the rise and fall of a chest no longer moved by the machine, a last fragile hope for a miracle we both know is not coming.

Our children stand either side of you now, tears running down your faces. The sun chooses that moment to flood the room, the light and warmth embracing you in my place. All three of you smile through your pain.

The light has appeared now and my mother has stepped through, gesturing for me to join her. I am torn between the people I love but know out parting is only temporary.

I look over my shoulder at my beautiful children and my soulmate as they wrap their arms around each other, a family united in grief, then I step forward and feel the warmth of a new sun and begin my waiting.

THE BLUEBELL WOODS

She tiptoes through the fragile stems. She is so careful not to trample a single one under her dainty feet, though in reality, she merely stirs them, as a summer breeze might as it brushes against them. She knows the pain of being crushed, of being snapped. At times her anger builds and she could rip them out by their slender stalks, tear their roots from the ground and destroy their delicate beauty. She knows she could never do this, she above all knows how precious life is.

She pauses.

In a short time, the sunrise will begin slowly. Its fiery tendrils reaching out in the distance, lighting up the sky.

He is there.

He is always there.

Each night he sits surrounded by bowing beauties. Their heads hung in silent slumber. In a few hours they will raise their heads to the light as she slips back into the dark. She wishes he would leave. She wishes she could stop his nocturnal visits. She has tugged at his hair, scratched at his arms. Each attempt as ineffective as that first time. She never knew hate before. She knows she can never stop him. She hates that she cannot save those who will join her, and every night she remains alone, she rejoices.

She feels the pull.

A connection with the earth that tells her it is time.

She slips silently past him. He looks up as if he sees her but she knows he sees nothing.

He stands now and she freezes. He brushes himself down and walks away with that smile upon his face. She wants to rush towards him rip that smile from his face but knows she cannot. She is the one who put it there though not by choice. She looks down at the place he has vacated. The crumpled remnants of fragile life broken and twisted. She hopes they will recover but knows for some, like herself there is no amount of healing that can bring them back.

She takes one last look at the moon as it slips across the sky. Until tonight she must go. She has tried fighting it before holding on to see the sun just one more time but she does not have the strength. She takes one last breath tasting the night air, though it will never really fill her lungs again, an echo of the last one her tiny body took, though by then she had already left it. The air is polluted by his presence, like everything that remains behind, left in his wake. She feels herself sinking as she slides into the earth.

She curls around her bones. Anchored like a ship in harbour. Only he knows she is here and he still will not leave her in peace. Her thoughts begin to jumble, she cannot think, she cannot remember how long she has lain here. Her mind has blocked so much of that night to protect her; she wonders sometimes if she let herself remember, would that be enough to let her leave this place, but she does not feel strong enough. As time passes the memories drift further away from her, like a mist on the horizon.

Before the darkness takes her, she whispers a prayer, the same one always.

"Please Daddy find me, take me home but if you can't please let me wake alone."

The cooling of the earth stirs her and even before she rises she knows this night is different. She does not immediately rise as she would normally, eager to be free from the cold earth, instead she remains frozen, paralysed by fear.

She can hear him, and he is not alone.

She can hear that same soothing tone that lured her here all that time ago, coaxing her into grasping range.

He had been holding a rabbit, a wild created, wide eyed with terror. She remembered how its leg had been hanging down, she didn't think for one second at the time to question his explanation that he had found it that way, and wanted to help it. Both she and the rabbit had been so innocent and naïve.

He had asked her to help him, if she would just hold the rabbit for him, he could use some sticks, and the handkerchief peeping out of his jacket pocket, to make a splint to hold it still, he would be able to take the creature home and set its bone properly.

She had been fascinated by those bright eyes and the soft fur, she did not even remember taking those fateful steps that closed the space between them, her hand outstretched towards it.

Her fingers had barely brushed the fur before, she watched in horror, as he cast aside the animal and, his hands that had held the animal so gently, clamped onto her arms. One hand reached for the handkerchief and he had pressed it over her face. The acrid smell of it burnt her throat and stung her eyes, she had gagged as she struggled to free herself, inwardly screaming though no sound had escaped her lips. Then the darkness had engulfed her and everything went black.

She didn't want to remember, she tried to force the memories away again, but the floodgates once opened, could not be closed. She had to remember now, relive the pain, she could not understand why, but instinctively she knew there was a reason.

She recalled how, it was the terrible pain tearing through her entire body, that had brought her back from the dark that night. She remembered the sky was orange and red, the colours seemed so much brighter than any sunset she had seen before or since, it had been like nature was reflecting the flames that burnt through her.

Despite her pain, her confused mind held the image of the rabbit, and she had tried to turn her head, searching for the injured creature. That was when he had realised she was now conscious and the smile had appeared on his face. Her arms had flailed at him; she had tried digging her tiny fingernails into his arms, wishing her mother had not trimmed them only ours earlier. The more she had struggled, the more she had tried to fight him off, the wider his smile had grown. She snapped her teeth at him, trying to bite, to sink her teeth into the face that loomed over hers, her teeth clashed against each other as they only cut through the air.

Then his face had changed, no, it hadn't been his face, it was his eyes, they had gone blank, they turned black and hardened, and then, she felt his full weight bear down on her.

The pain, him on top of her, his hands devouring her flesh. She knew she had screamed at that point, screamed in pain, in terror, a scream that had torn at her throat and lungs with its intensity, before his hand made contact with the side of her head, and the darkness had consumed her once more.

The darkness had been different this time; it had been like a fog surrounding her. Everything was muffled, she had found herself standing up, and she could recall she had tried running away, but had been unable to move. It had been then she had looked down at her feet, and see the rabbit laying in the grass, its head twisted at an angle which left no doubt that it was dead.

Then she had seen everything.

She remembered standing, and watching him do things she did not understand to her body, she knew that what he was doing was wrong, but there was nothing she could do to stop him. Random thoughts had entered her mind, she had thought how angry her mum would be over the dirt smeared on her white knee socks, she noticed one of the ribbons was missing from her hair and wondered where it was. She had been thankful that she could no longer feel the pain he was inflicting upon her.

It had seemed to last forever, she watched as her body took its last breath. She wondered why she was here watching, at school they told you that when you died you went to heaven, but she was still here, watching the bad man kill her, had she been bad? Did the fact she was watching mean that she had done something wrong? Maybe she had to wait until he finished for the angels to come.

That was what she had thought then, but now, she realised that no one was going to come for her, she had to wait here until she had done something, there was something she had to do, first she had to remember, then she had to do, do what? She still did not know what the something was.

He had been sweating and she remembered thinking how horrible it would be making her pretty dress as it dripped own onto it. She recalled how his grunting had got louder and louder. She had looked round at that point, convinced someone must hear him and come to save her, make him get off her. Then suddenly he was still.

He had slowly climbed to his feet and stood looking down at her. Then he had straightened his clothes and turned his back on her. She had watched as he pulled out a packet of cigarettes, cursing that his packet had been crushed before pulling one out and lighting it.

For the first time she looked round and realised she was lost. She had no idea where she was, she had never been here before, and wondered how her mummy and daddy would find her. It was then she looked at her own body again, the neck bent at an angle mirroring that of the rabbit. There was blood streaked down her legs, and soaking her dress. She had known he had done something bad to her, though she could never have given a name to the act, but with a child's innocence it was the sight of her new dress ruined, that hit home.

Then a totally irrational fear had gripped her, she had been scared she would be in trouble with her mummy, she had been bad after all, she knew she wasn't supposed to wander off. She had known she wasn't supposed to go out of the garden, and definitely not go down the lane into the field. Her daddy would be cross, they were supposed to be going out, but she had been bored waiting, while they were arguing, she had known they were arguing, the closed door never fooled her.

The man had moved then. He had collected a spade that had been resting against a tree, and he had begun digging, her little mind raced, then she realised what he intended to do.

Voiceless, she screamed. No!

Eventually she'd stood transfixed, watching as the hole grew bigger, until finally he seemed satisfied with its depth. He stood with his back to her for what seemed like an age, looking down at her body, he was making the strange grunting noise again, but other than the slight movement of one shoulder, he appeared to be still.

After another few minutes he bent over and grabbed her ankles, and the thought had flitted through her mind about whether they were still her ankles now she was no longer in the body, horrified she watched as he hoisted her up. Her dress had fallen over her head and face as he swung her towards the hole. She saw her body fall in a strange heap, arms and legs tangled in what seemed like an impossible position, then he turned and bent again, the flash of fur through the air distracted her for a fraction of a second, before the broken body of the rabbit, landed on hers.

She had no idea how she had moved but she had thrown herself against his bulk, beating down on his back as he bent shovelling dirt over the evidence of his depravity. For a brief moment she almost believed he had felt her, he had brushed away at the area where her tiny fists struck, but it was no more than brushing away a speck of dust.

Finally, she had dropped to the grass, watching as the earth claimed her for its own, when he had finished, he re-covered the area with the clods of turf. Dissatisfied with the effect, he looked round and saw the fallen tree, a victim of a recent thunderstorm. He hauled it over, using it to cover the broken ground he rearranged its limbs until he was convinced one corpse disguised the resting place of the other.

Once more he lit another cigarette. She watched as smoke curled against the flaming sunset until he dropped the stub, and with his toe, he ground it into the leaves and the earth below.

As he turned to walk away she saw it, a pink silken ribbon, snaking from his pocket, her ribbon.

His trophy.

It had been at that moment when she had felt the pull for the first time, and her silent screams had echoed in her head as she was drawn down into her bones deep beneath the cold, dark soil.

It was the screams now that forced the memories away, though it seemed like an age, she knew that all she had remembered, she had experienced in a moment, not like the day it had happened to her when it had lasted an eternity.

Her worst fears had come true and she listened to the sobs of the frightened child. He has brought another child here, here where her bones lay. She wants to stay and hide, not to witness the horror she knows will play out above if she cannot stop it. She thinks of her mummy and daddy; how sad they would have been when they realised she was gone. She cannot stop her parents pain but, she can stop another set of parents feeling the same.

She knows she must act now.

She cannot wait any longer if she wishes to save girl, though how she will achieve this she has no idea. It is not yet sunset, not her normal hour to rise from the earth, but the bond with the crying girl draws her and gives her strength. Her journey from her bones to the surface seems to take forever, though in fact it takes no longer than the thought of moving from one to the other. As her eyes adjust to the faint light which blinds her momentarily as she emerges from the darkness, she takes in the scene before her.

The girl is a little older than she was, and she senses he has brought her here rather than stumbled across her, the pale evening light shows the tear stains on the girl's face, she is bound and the bruise at her temple suggests, she too has tasted the darkness. He is the same as he ever was, a sheen of sweat seeps from his brow and she is aware of the smell, a smell she has tried so hard to forget sweat cigarettes and the other substance she cannot name.

The girl cowers against the dead log, the rotting carcass of a tree dragged there many years ago, the carpet of blue that has sprung up around it, is now trampled and crushed. She tries to curl up so small as to become invisible, but it makes no difference. The pleasure he takes from her fear is obvious.

She looks round for a way to stop what she knows will come next, she screams at the man to get away from the girl, and at the girl to be brave, and hold on, she watches him close the space between himself and his victim.

In the distance she hears a dog bark.

He does not hear it, he is consumed by his own lust, the girl hears nothing to, but that is because he struck her and the darkness has engulfed her once more, it delays his pleasure though, he explores her body as he awaits her return to consciousness. She knows time is running out.

She gathers all her energy and forces herself towards the animal by the sheer force of will. The dog, some form of terrier, is engrossed in sniffing in the undergrowth a distance away, it takes so much from her to reach so far away from her bones. The dog's owner is even further away but it is not his attention she needs, once the dog runs he will follow, of this she has no doubt.

She flies at the dog, creating an invisible whirlwind around it to distract it from the scent of rabbits. The dog leaps in the air snapping at the invisible foe, and as it does so she fills its nostrils with the scent of her bones, she hopes that it will be enough to lure him from his previous exploration. The owner is closing the distance between them now, she knows she must act quickly, if he gets the lead on the dog all would be lost. She allows the pull of the bones to take her back, giving just enough resistance to make sure the dog comes with them, tantalised by the possibility of a bone to gnaw upon.

The dog eagerly continues, his owner following and cursing under his breath, the act of running after the dog has robbed him of his voice. It is a lucky break, she thinks, she had not considered the man might be alerted, she hopes he will be too consumed in his own thoughts and not hear them approach, it is not enough to save the girl, he must be seen, be known, be stopped for good.

She can see them on the ground as she draws nearer, his bulk on top moving on the obscured figure she knows lies beneath, she worries she is already too late, and at that moment she watches in horror as a figure rises from the ground and stands looking confused.

Two pairs of spectral eyes connect and there is understanding, it is not yet too late, it is the pain that has driven her from the flesh, but the blood has not yet stopped pumping. The dog bursts through the bushes, his yapping transforms to growling as it stops short of where the man sweats and grunts on the ground, where the promised bones are buried.

The spirits connect as one descends back into the flesh, she knows the girl need only hold on a little longer for rescue, the man has stopped now, shocked by the appearance of the dog. He does not have time to gather his thoughts before the dog owner appears and recognition at what they are witnessing shows in both men's faces.

The dog owner wears a mask of horror at the scene he has come upon, the other man realises he has been caught, for a moment she feels fear for the man she has lured here, that the predator will turn and attack but he does not get chance. The dog walker is quicker, he grabs a nearby branch and it is the man who enters the darkness this time, when he re-emerges he will find he has been bound with the same ties he used on the girl, and the dog lead.

The dog walker rips off his coat and wraps it round the girl, at the same time, he has his phone in his hand, garbled messages of depravity and lost innocence drift across invisible currents, and she hopes help will not be long.

The two girls are staring at each other one trying to remain in the damaged body and the other willing her there, if one can save the other they will both be free.

Sirens rip through the air, the ghost girls grasp on the other slips away as professionals step in to stem the bleeding, and begin the process of healing the flesh, the heart she knows will never really heal but she will live and love, surrounded by parents that will never know just how close they came to losing her. She is sure the girl will never tell of her presence, if she did she would not be believed, but it does not matter all that matters is that she has been saved.

She watches as the woman in uniform wraps a protective arm around the other girl's shoulder. They have worked on her for several minutes before preparing to move her, her soul is finally tethered once more inside the flesh, she no longer see the girl who pushed her back in and held her hand. She tries to speak, to tell before she forgets but the mask over her face is making her drowsy and they hush her to a peaceful slumber.

The man is now hauled to his feet, despite everything, he looks towards the girl, and to the log, and the smile still comes. His capture is not enough, his memories will keep his smile in place. As he is dragged away, hands cuffed behind his back, something falls from his pocket, a tattered, slither of pink silk which tangles in amongst the blue blooms. A policeman picks it up and places is in a plastic bag, a memory triggered but he cannot think what it is just yet.

The dog owner now returns his attention to his charge who he tied to the rotting log out of the way. He intends to praise his companion for bringing him to this spot but he is busy searching out his prize. The dog owner calls out bringing attention to the spot where the dog has begun the excavations in his determination to reach the bones he knows lie beneath. With every inch the dog digs she feels the hold the bones have upon her is fading, one final paw full thrown in the air before the indignant animal is hauled away, yapping in his frustration.

From the ground, a second slither of tattered pink silk now shows, and the policeman goes noticeably paler before voices once more erupt across the airwaves, she does not understand the significance of the message, but knows her release is coming.

She stands as men in plastic suits arrive and surround the hole on hands and knees, more sirens sound, more people arrive, activity a short distance away. The ambulance adds it siren to the cacophony as it moves away rushing the girl she has saved to safety.

Chaos and confusion as figures break through the tape that someone has stretched in a circle enclosing half of the field. She realises she is finding it harder to focus, glancing up she see sunset has finished, yet she knows she will not return to the bones with the sunrise. A shriek draws her attention to a woman, she has let out the most terrible heart wrenching sound, if her heart had still been beating, that one single moment, that sound, would have stopped it.

They are older, visibly older, grey hair streaks the blonde cascade she remembers tangling her fingers through. The man grabbing the woman, holding her back, has a stick, he leans on it now with one hand, while the other clutches his wife. The policeman walks towards them, plastic shielding the exhibit from the tears which will drop on it in a minute. He holds it out for confirmation of what they all know; heads nod before the couple explode in sobs that shake their bodies.

Raised voices behind her make her turn, a signal announcing the first of her bones as it emerges from the earth, she needed no sign, she can feel a warmth as the sun touches her body for the first time in years.

With the touch of the sun the hold her bones have upon her dissipates, she knows she is free to leave, but she cannot go yet. She approaches the couple as they cling together in grief, relief and more conflicting emotions than they can put names to. The woman's hand hangs limp by her side, she is drained of all strength, help up by the husband she has alternately clung to and berated in the past ten years.

The girl slips her hand into her mothers, she notices how those once perfectly manicured nails have been ravaged, they are now ragged and bitten down.

She closes her eyes and wills the woman to feel her there, and for one precious moment, her mother looks down at her, mother and daughter connected in a way that neither death nor time can erode.

A whisper.

"Emily."

Her hand slips from her mother's grasp as the light envelops her. Other loving arms reach out and gather her to them, to take her away from the pain. She can wait in peace now until they are all reunited once more.

WAKE ME UP

Bleep. Bleep. Bleep.

The last thing the Captain said to me was wake me up if you have any problems. Well, as that immortal quote goes, *Houston we have a problem*, in fact, at this point a problem is just about the only thing we do have.

So yes, in theory, I should be waking the Captain, and everyone else, up instead of sitting here recording this message, but maybe, once you hear our situation, you will understand why I have chosen this course of action.

I am the ship's doctor Lt Anna Lucas, and I am going to try to remain as calm as I can while I explain our situation and the decision I have reached. At the end of this you may feel I have overstepped my authority, but I ask you, if you were here, standing in my shoes, would you do things differently? But of course, I am getting ahead of myself, you can't answer that yet.

We are the scientific research ship NC-Nightingale, we left the moon base almost three Earth years ago on a journey to an exploration platform in the Elthanor Nebula. I do wonder at times who chooses these names but that is irrelevant and I must try to focus on giving you just the facts. We are a crew of eight and in order to minimise the amount of supplies we carry, most of the journey is spent in stasis. There is the Captain, Richard Devlin he has been serving longer than any of us, myself, two engineers and four scientist specialising in different fields.

We were heading to the platform with the expectation of remaining there for the foreseeable future. At this time Earth has only decades left where it can safely sustain life, many have already evacuated to the Moon base and to the recently set up colonies on Mars, but they cannot provide for the entire population long term. The hope was the platform would allow for further exploration to find a suitable planet for habitation, either naturally or via biospheres, I guess that hope is now lost.

The advances in bioengineering ironically have contributed to our situation, in the old days we would have had to carry extra supplies for the platform but is no longer necessary. Other than the genetically modified seeds specially designed for growth in artificial environments we carry nothing to them, the platforms are all self-sufficient. Somewhere drifting out there is enough food to feed us a hundred times over, but again I am drifting. I need to focus, explain myself properly, not let the rising tide, no, I'm not going there, where was I?

Ah yes, so, the first week out we are all awake, carrying out all the checks and ensuring all equipment is functioning fully, of course this is all done prior to take off as well but sometimes you just can't tell how new equipment is going to handle the pressure, the only thing that failed us this trip was the coffee machine, not something to abandon a voyage over, but right now I could do with one.

After all checks are done and experiments set up, then the Captain sets the auto-pilot. He sets the course, back up protocols and checks all the emergency systems, and then I take the first watch. People are always surprised about that; they assume it would be the Captain but I always take the first month long solo watch to ensure that the stasis chambers all function properly. I monitor all the chambers and make adjustments based on the individual's readings. Everyone handles stasis differently, but these days there are few side effects and, given the rotation system we use it avoids some of those, such as muscle wastage during sleep cycles, that plagued those who came before us.

Really there is not much to do other than watch movies and read during the waking month. We perform regular checks on the instruments, keep an eye on any ongoing experiments set running at departure and generally listen out for any alarms.

Then the final day of the month we change over, the advances in stasis mean it only now takes two hours to bring someone out from sleep mode and around thirty minutes for total immersion into it. So for sixteen hours you have contact with another human before taking your place in sleep mode. Not only does this save on the amount of physical rations that need to be carried but also means on a trip like this no one really ages more than a few months in transit.

Of course the not ageing part can have side effects on relationships, which is why the company chooses only single personnel for these missions. It is hard enough being apart for years at a time, but to return, then find your other half looks a few years older than you, does not always go down well. Not an issue we have to worry about now, and at least there are no husbands and wives, sat waiting for messages that might never come. But there I go again, racing ahead, and really there is no need to, not now.

Four weeks ago the Captain woke me, it was round to my turn again and we were close to our destination, normally he may have even have considered staying awake for the last few weeks. We were due to arrive at the platform in around five weeks from that point, but our ration supply seemed a lot lower than it should have been. I knew this was down to Harris, one of the engineers.

As I monitored the stasis chambers during my shifts, I had found I had to adjust his several times, due to a gain in weight, where as everyone else had lost a couple of pounds, but at this point, I chose not to mention that to the Captain. He would see if for himself once everyone was awake. Or he would have.

To be fair to Harris, the machines also picked up on a growth which had developed during the course of our journey, this probably accounted for him feeling hungrier than usual. I had considered waking him to discuss it, but had decided not to. Instead I set his chamber to run extra scans and tests, to monitor the growth, with the intention of operating, once we reached the platform.

The ship has a basic medical bay but is not really equipped for performing surgery in flight and I also have to say a part of me was curious, whatever this growth was, it continued to grow while in stasis when really it should have halted its progress, I wanted to be able to examine it further under the proper condition. If I had believed he was in danger, I would have woken him, and operated in a heartbeat, please, don't doubt that.

The problem is we are a week out from the platform and I should be able to see it on the horizon. Instead all I see is a steady stream of debris floating in space. I have tried to make radio contact but all there is… is static, the steady drone of white noise. I might not be as experienced as some of the other crew members but I know we do not have enough fuel to make it home.

If we were close enough to make contact with Earth or the Moon Base, it might be worth waking people and giving them the chance to send a message home. A chance to say goodbye before we run out of supplies, and die slowly of hunger, before any rescue could reach us.

I have tried every wavelength possible in the hope of finding a satellite or another ship, anything to bounce a signal off, but nothing. I have scanned the horizon looking for escape pods, shuttles, the slightest sign that anyone on the platform made it off. There were five hundred people living and working there, and now they are all gone,

I have no idea what has happened to the platform, I can only speculate some form of explosion has torn the place apart, but what caused it will probably never be known, unless they had chance to send out a message, before whatever did happen happened. That is really our only hope; that they sent out a distress call and someone rushing to their aid, might come across us as we sleep.

Even as I record this I wonder if I really have the right to make this choice, but after considering every possibility, I decided this is not just our best chance, it is our only chance. I have to hope the platform sent out a distress signal before it exploded, that somewhere out there a rescue team is already on route, not for us, but for them, and that they will find us. I don't know if I am doing the right thing, if I even have the right to make this choice.

I have reprogrammed the auto pilot to head for the nearest inhabited planet, we do not have enough fuel to reach it but if we are lucky we may cross the path of another ship and they may hear the distress message I have begun broadcasting on all frequencies. Once I have finished recording this, I will head to my own stasis chamber, and auto induce my own sleep. If we are not rescued then we will perish without knowing our own fate, I have taken the decision that this is better than being awake but entirely unable to alter the situation.

    I am staring out now, watching pieces of the debris as they drift aimlessly, I swear I saw a shoe, just one single shoe, is that all that is left to show for the life that bustled around that platform? Would that be better to go suddenly?

    After I made the call I realised that there was a fault with my plan, once the engines and power cut out the stasis chambers would automatically reboot to revive us all. I have reprogrammed them to, I can't even say it, let's just say we will not wake to find ourselves in a mausoleum in space. We will not emerge to suffocate from lack of oxygen as the life support systems fail. I might not have the right, there will be some who say I am playing God, others will call me a murderer, but I ask you now you know, know what we face, what would you do?

    I am scared, even now, when I have made my decision, I hesitate. Ask anyone to lay down in their tomb and await death and I am pretty sure the words go to hell will come flying back at you, yet that is exactly what I must force myself to do. And if I stop, for just one minute, to think of the bigger picture, of what this all means, then the breath is forced from my lungs as I gasp for air, knuckles white as I desperately hold myself up.

You see even as I record this, I know what it will mean if you are listening to this, that you too are probably in the same position as we are now. You too will be miles from home, heading to a place that no longer exists, without enough food for your own crew, never mind a bunch of strangers, frozen and drifting in space.

And now you have listened to this I have put you in an even more painful position than the one I am in, and for that I am truly sorry, I really am. I don't know what to say to you, I would not, will not, cannot hold it against you if you put your own crew first and pretend you never heard this message. I cannot forgive myself for the thought that I am making you make that choice, that my voice will haunt you when you have no options.

I don't want to die, I had so many things I wanted to do. I always thought that I would be brave in the face of death, that if I was going to die it would be doing something heroic, but no, the chances are I will slip away unnoticed, isolated in a cocoon designed to preserve life. All I can do now is hope and pray as I fall asleep that someone, anyone hears this before it is too late and that they have the chance to wake me up.

Bleep. Bleep. Bleep.

Removing his headset Stephan turned to his crewmate, a puzzled expression on his face.

"I just listened to a distress message."

"So? You want to set co-ordinates and go have a look?"

"That's the thing, I know there is nothing to go find."

"What you on about, distress signal equals either rescue or salvage, either way we make a profit, so load up the co-ordinates and let's hustle."

Stephen shook his head, well aware that his crew mate would think him mad, but he could think of no way to explain the message he had just heard.

"You remember back in school we were taught in history about the first lunar settlers and the exploration quests that were sent out?"

"Vaguely, school was more your thing, that's why you have the qualifications and do the flying bit, and why I rely on the family funds to fuel the engines."

"NC-Nightingale, what does that mean to you?"

"Nothing! Should it?"

Stephen paused trying to work out the best way to explain things, Mike was a nice guy but it was true he had not paid any attention in school, he knew he didn't have to, salvage was big business and his family ran the biggest interstellar salvage outfit in this quadrant.

"NC-Nightingale was one of the first exploration ships, it disappeared just after the science station it was heading towards was blasted out of space at the start of the first Interplanetary War."

"So it's old salvage, hit in the numbers."

"Not old, impossible. It has been over five hundred years, even if it was floating around out there intact, there is no way that it would have enough power to be sending that message."

"What are you on about?"

"I have just listened to a woman from over five hundred years ago, sending a message there is no way I should be able to hear."

"Yeah right, of course you did, you're hearing dead women? You expect me to believe that?"

"Here listen for yourself."

Stephen passed Mike the headphones and watched the colour drain from his face as the message began to replay again.

THE ANNIVERSARY

She checked her watch, she was early but that was okay she would rather hang around than risk missing him. She pulled her coat tighter round her, despite the mild day it had turned bitterly cold once the sun had retreated. She recalled the first time she had come here, it had been in the harsh grey light of a November morning, bleak and desolate or maybe that had been her feelings projected onto the landscape.

She felt the usual panic building, the fear he would not come, that she would be left waiting. It was always the same, always had been, the fear he would leave her that one day he would not come. She had always found it so hard to believe he had loved her, that he had seen something within her worthy of him, she had spent hours staring in the mirror searching for the elusive something that made him love her.

The first time she had ever looked into his eyes it had been liking coming home, a collision in the supermarket, spilled groceries from both baskets mixed on the floor had signalled the beginning of her life, before she had merely existed. She tried to remember life before their hands had touched as he passed her back a tin of beans, all she found was a blurred merry-go-round of work, ready meals and mindless hours wasted staring at the TV.

He had given her life meaning, he still did, and she couldn't bear the thought of life without his presence even if it was not the happy ending she still dreamed of.

She checked her watch again, any time now he would be here, she wondered what she would do if he did not show. Could she turn and walk away back to the life she had endured before? Would she find the courage to go look for him, to search him out? She had considered that before

She watched as he appeared, her breath caught in her throat as he approached the bridge from the opposite side and stopped the centre. The overcoat she had given him for his birthday caught the wind and billowed out as he placed his briefcase on the ground next to him. She walked towards him a sad smile forming as the tears began to roll down her cheeks. A few feet from him she stopped.

My love.

He looked round now, she saw the fear and panic in his eyes, this was always the hardest part, the assault by unseen assailants. She watched as his body convulsed under a barrage of invisible fists before the moment. It was this moment that dragged her back each time, his back pressed against the barricade he glanced over his shoulder, down into the inky darkness.

Time seemed to freeze for an eternity but was really only the passing of a moment, then he looked up, looked straight at her, mouth opening issuing words she would never hear. Then like he was swept up by a blast of the icy wind he flew backwards disappearing into the swirling current below.

Stifling her sobs she stepped forward to where he had been only seconds before and stretching out a gloved hand let the flower she had been clutching fall from her hand. Crumpled and broken from the vice like grip she had exerted on it, it followed the line of his descent.

"Until next year my love."

She turned and left, not lingering as she had the first time, he would not return and neither would she until the next anniversary.

THE LAST WORD

You always said I would be late for my own funeral, and in a way, that was true, my body was at least, though to be honest time has little meaning to me any longer. You pride yourself on always being right, and so many times it turned out to be annoyingly true.

You sat by my bedside long after I had departed, tears stained your face despite knowing, as we both did inside, it was a blessed release. You had been the rock that had anchored me in those final months, and a thousand other clichés, as the cancer had ravaged my body. You had lied and told me I still looked beautiful, you were very convincing, but the pain behind your eyes would always give you away.

You cared for me after I could no longer thank you, knowing me well enough to know the gratitude I would have expressed, had I been able, that it was you and not a stranger who brushed my hair each morning and wiped my face. Even when there were things you could not do, you were there 'supervising', your favourite phrase rather than admitting yourself incapable of anything.

You had taken control at the end, made calls, ensured those who needed to have a last visit had made it in time. You made sure I looked as good as possible and I was thankful for that, it saved extra pain for my friends and allowed me a last shred of dignity, despite the diseases best efforts. At that point I was still in my body, unresponsive, but aware of all that was happening.

You knew the second I left, not from the last rattling breath, but because I brushed against your cheek with my lips as I rose from the flesh. A cold breeze that your hand lifted as if to catch. Tears had flowed down your cheeks, but a smile flitted across your lips knowing I was free and could no longer feel the pain, and that no more indignities awaited me, but rather I could fly, and run, and dance once more.

So many people are gathered here to watch what remains of the body that failed me be disposed of, I thought it would bother me, that I would feel a sense of loss, or pain, but I feel neither anymore, only joy and love.

I feel the love that floods this building, love not only for me but for all of you, my friends, my family, even the dog. I have visited so many times in this last week while you all talked flowers and hymns in between the tears, I am sure only the dog sensed my presence the majority of the time. Once I thought you knew I was by your side, you looked straight at me, a smile laying on your lips before the tears flowed once more and you buried your face in your hands.

I wanted so badly to comfort you but I cannot. I would wrap my arms around you if I could, take away your pain, but that would not be fair either, for through the pain you will realise your strength and let others see where I got mine from. I was not brave and courageous alone, you stood beside me and gave me strength when I needed it, carrying me when I could no longer take the next step.

So many people lament the life cut short, the things I will never do or see, but they are wrong. I wish I could show you the world I see now, I can go anywhere, see anything, I can dance amongst the stars, watch the sun rise and set over any shore, but my favourite place remains by your side.

Sometimes I leave clues, things I know you see, things I know make you think of me, and I hope in time that the tears will dry and that smile I love so well will return to where it belongs.

Everyone says they are here to say goodbye, but we never do, not really, it is only a temporary parting until we meet again. I want to let you know I am here with you on this most difficult of days, to let you know I stand by you in your hour of need, as you stood by me, but I do not have the strength to make my presence felt.

The whispers build as you prepare to give your speech, you stand there looking so pale, my passing has aged you in ways that the illness did not. While I was ill there was always hope, the prayer for a miracle, even if an answer was never expected, but death seems so final, and I suppose it is in some ways.

You will never hold that body again, never kiss that flesh, but when you close your eyes I will be waiting there, always, death cannot change that. I will come to you in dreams and we will walk hand in hand and talk, and it will never be quite enough, but, it will sustain us both until the day comes when you join me.

I move now and stand next to you as you talk about my life, my loss and all I meant to those gathered here. You leave the spaces between the lines for others to read, some things do not need to be said and there are no words adequate. Your hand shakes as you try to turn the paper with your scrawled notes upon it, I long to take it and hold it steady, to reassure you that you are doing me proud, you always have and always will.

It is nearly over now, you return to your seat, faltering slightly as you pass by my coffin, as coffins go you made a good choice, kept it simple and elegant, there are a few who thought it plain but you knew what was best suited to me. It fascinates me that a wooden box can inspire such emotion, a box is just a box, as a body is just a body, it is what is inside that is important, but maybe that only becomes clear after one is no longer confined. I know you know I am no longer there, not trapped and suffering in that body or that box, but your heart and mind are still at odds in accepting this. If logic ruled it would say I am not here by your side, yet here I remain.

Everyone stands and files past the coffin as they leave, in an ideal world I would have wanted a burial but if the world had been ideal we would not be here today at all. Lilies fragrance the air overpowering the white roses so many have chosen to leave alongside them.

In the hallway you stand shaking hands with all those who have attended, accepting the mumbled words, the spoken condolences mixed with silent thanks that it is not their loved one that is being mourned.

The guilt of the living is always there, some wish it had been them, usually those who it would have destroyed me to lose, or they wish the disease on others, as if it cares who it takes, as if goodness should be a protection. For so many their guilt is their relief, relief that their family is intact, that it is not they who are suffering. It is human nature, I would not wish anyone here to take my place, but I understand their feelings, and so do you; that is why you smile and accept the spoken words without hesitation.

You have invited close friends and family to a restaurant afterwards, some think this bad form that the doors are not flung open to all, but you understand the need for a private time for those closest to mourn.

More tears flow with the alcohol, smiles are recalled, funny stories and happy memories, and this is how I live on now. I live on because you speak my name, you remember me, my smile, my smell, and my quirks. In your dreams we talk but in your heart and on your tongue I live on into the present.

I will always be with you, will always watch over you. When you smile I will see what has made you happy, and it will make me happy, you will love once more, and I shall share your love, it will take nothing away from the love we shared. You will laugh and I will share your laughter but when you are sad I will feel your sadness, and it will break my heart, and I shall long to see you happy once more.

You can no longer see me but I can see you, and I will do all I can to let you know I am here. I watch as the tiny feather flutters down from nowhere to land in your glass, and I smile as you smile, because I know, you know, I am here.

ABOUT THE AUTHOR

Born in Leeds, currently living in Huddersfield, Paula Acton is many things, an author, a mother to two amazing kids, grandmother to two gorgeous little people, and a slave to a dog, and a cat. She also has two horses which she claims are cheaper and more effective than therapy.

She has a tendency to write fantasy with a dark twist but also writes the occasional romance after success in various anthologies trying out different genres.

When not writing she can frequently be found wandering around randomly with her camera or with her headphones in listening to True Crime Podcasts.

You can find out more on her on her various social media sites

Website - http://paulaacton.co.uk

Facebook - https://www.facebook.com/Paula.Acton.Author

Instagram - https://instagram.com/paulaacton/

Twitter – https://twitter.com/Paula_Acton

You can find the cover designers Melchelle Designs on social media at

Website - https://melchelledesigns.com/

Facebook - https://www.facebook.com/MelchelleDesigns/

Twitter – https://twitter.com/MelchelleDesign

And discover more about Charlie Harris-Beard and Cords4Life.uk here

Website – http://www.cords4life.co.uk/

Facebook – https://www.facebook.com/Cords4Life/

Paula Acton

Disintegration & Other Stories

What happens when the fairy tale turns sour?
When 'Happily Ever After' ends in tears?

Disintegration & Other Stories explores what happens when it all goes wrong,

Sometimes sad, sometimes humorous, and sometimes until death we do part takes on a whole new meaning.

A collection of short stories that will leave you wanting more…

Voices Across The Void

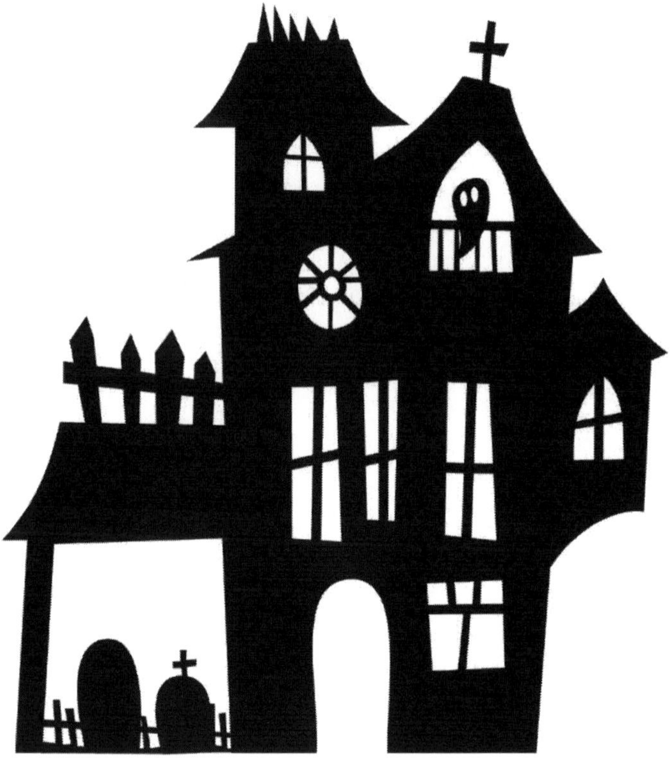

Voices Across The Void

Printed in Great Britain
by Amazon